**Why did he keep staring at her as if she were a piece of shoofly pie? And who was he, anyway?**

She drew her arm away. "Mr. Callahan, talking will do me no good. I am tired and dirty."

His face showed obvious compassion. Those eyes, targeting hers as surely as a dart. Did she play darts? Did her father, a man friend, a brother?

His hand nudged her arm. Not to be manhandled again, she jerked back.

"Mr. Callahan, the railroad is putting us up in the hotel across the street. Tomorrow I intend to speak with a doctor." She'd speak with anyone at all to discover who she was. "If you'll excuse me." She took a shaky step but stopped soon enough.

"Rebecca. I'm here because we're supposed to be married tomorrow."

"Married?" Head whirling, she felt her eyes flutter as he grabbed her to him.

**Books by Linda S. Glaz**

Love Inspired Heartsong Presents

*With Eyes of Love*
*Always, Abby*
*The Substitute Bride*

## LINDA S. GLAZ

Linda, married with three grown children and three grandchildren, is a complete triple-A personality. How else would she find time to write as well as be an agent for Hartline Literary Agency? She loves any and everything about the written word and loves families passing stories along through the generations. If she isn't writing or putting together a contract, you'll find her taking a relaxing bath with her eReader in hand.

# LINDA S. GLAZ

# *The Substitute Bride*

HEARTSONG
PRESENTS

Recycling programs
for this product may
not exist in your area.

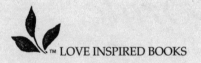 ™ LOVE INSPIRED BOOKS

ISBN-13: 978-0-373-48669-4

THE SUBSTITUTE BRIDE

www.LoveInspiredBooks.com

Printed in U.S.A.

A man's heart plans his way,
but the Lord determines his steps.
—*Proverbs* 16:9

To my cousin Patty Adams for sticking with me
four years as I finally got the vision for this story,
and to Kathy Henry, her sister and my other cuz, for
brainstorming two of the tough sections with us. You
two are closer to me than any sister could be and I'm
so grateful to God for putting us in the same family.
Love you guys…

# Chapter 1

There was no sound but that of crickets and whooshing horse tails. Tired of standing in the hot September sun battling swarms of flies, the horses swished their tails to the rhythm of the insects' chirps and stomped their feet to signal *let's go.*

Jared Callahan massaged the back of his neck as he strained to hear the train whistle. He, too, had waited in the sweltering heat longer than expected, and the flies irritated him nearly as much. He brushed one from the perfume-scented paper he'd just finished reading once again.

> *I'll be arriving at eleven in the morning on the tenth. I hope you'll be anxiously awaiting my train. Yours lovingly, Rebecca Layne.*
>
> *Yours lovingly.*

Swiping sweat from his eyes, he slid off the wooden bench and returned to the building where Bobby Reed, the stationmaster in too-long sleeves and a canvas vest, apologized one more time. "Not sure why the train's late. But I'll let you know soon as I have word."

Jared shoved past the other anxious folks and moved back to the bench. Opening the letter again, he allowed the words to sink into his heart. Gently sloping script filled the page as well as the sides. He reread the last sentence for the fourth time since arriving in town, thinking he might have misunderstood the day or hour. No matter how many times he scanned the words, they said the same thing.

Uh-uh. No misunderstanding. She said lovingly and she meant it. His mail-order bride would arrive, throw her arms around him and they would be married. Just like that.

The noon sun bore down on him, sweat mingling with the dust from the ride into town. He slipped off his hat, ran a hand through damp hair that he recognized as long overdue for cutting and stared over the open prairie toward the lure of his homestead. The hot, miserable Minnesota summer choked him with the sun's last chance to make him almost wish for winter. But he couldn't think about that now. All he thought about was his beautiful Rebecca.

"Young fella?" Reed's nasally voice penetrated Jared's daydreams. "I hate to be the one to break it to ya, but I just got word. The train you're waiting for derailed some distance this side of Rochester. A lot of folks injured."

Jared jumped from the seat. "They what?"

"Calm down. That's all I know for now. Hopefully,

I'll have more information in a bit. Why don't you stroll across the street to Millie's and get yourself a sarsaparilla? I'll come find you when I get more particulars."

Jared glanced across the narrow street toward Millie's. Uh-uh. He'd wait right here. With a quick crease, he refolded the wrinkled paper and slid the letter into his pocket. She might be dead. After all their plans, she could have been killed in a train accident. He slapped his hat against the bench.

Not acceptable. Surely God wouldn't allow his future bride to die.


The wagon bounced over the rutted road until she longed to rub her backside for relief. Empty prairie for miles and an occasional scrub of trees that dotted the land here and there. Looking across the wagon, she recognized the man who'd offered her his coat following the accident. He was sitting directly across from her. She grew uneasy under his scrutiny. He eyed her as if he could read the doubts in her mind, and she quickly diverted her gaze.

Over the side of the wagon, ash swirled around the horses' hooves. This far away and still the burning followed them.

She leaned toward an older woman at her side. "Where do you suppose they will take us?"

A grunt and a dazed expression emanated from her riding companion.

Another scan of the wagon box provided nothing more than that man's glare closing in on her once again. Only this time, it made her more than a bit uncomfortable. Why didn't he look elsewhere?

They hit a bump and she slid forward, slamming

her knee into Mr. Fletcher. He cocked a grin in her direction and she scrambled back to her post next to the gray-haired lady. For some reason, her skin crawled.

If only she could remember who she was and where she'd come from.

Even more important…where she was going.

Tired as all get out, Jared leaned his head against the side of the false building front and pulled his hat over his face. The stationmaster said wagons should start arriving soon. What was taking them so long? He'd been in town all afternoon. At home there would be one very angry cow if it weren't for a nearly weaned calf no doubt helping herself to the extra milk.

Would Rebecca be among those living or among the dead? He closed his eyes and prayed for sleep to release him from worry. She had to be alive. He'd pinned all his hopes on her.

The sound of teams of horses awakened him. He leaped up, scanning the muddled scene unfolding before him. A hundred feet or so of wagons filled with folks seemingly in a daze, lined the town front to back and then some.

One by one the folks climbed out of the wagons with the help of townspeople. A handful of womenfolk cried; others groaned. What had happened out there? The stationmaster shouted out names. A stout man nursing a slight limp moved toward the second-to-last wagon and helped a young woman from the back.

Jared's back stiffened. Curly blond hair, wide blue eyes and a rather curvy figure caught his attention at once. Alone, the lady stepped around the wagon wheel and gazed toward the crowd of people, no doubt scanning the group for him.

Jared pushed through the throng of people and edged forward, touching her arm. "Miss Layne?"

She turned toward his voice. Dirt smudged her cheek and a goose egg bulged from her temple—she was injured! He should have been there to protect her.

"Rebecca Layne? I'm Jared Callahan. I believe you're looking for me." He put his hand out but she pulled away.

"Layne?" She hesitated to offer her hand, indecision lining her face with worry. "You are waiting for me? I'm afraid I don't know anyone here."

He glanced at the beautiful face again, streaked with sooty smudges. He hadn't noticed any other young ladies alight from the wagons. This had to be Rebecca. She fit her description perfectly, right down to the dark blue skirt and white blouse she said she'd be wearing.

"Can I help you with your things?"

"I don't have any *things*." She drew back, the blue eyes sparkling with what? Frustration or fear? "I'm sorry, Mr. Callahan, was it? You must be mistaken. I don't know any Rebecca Layne."

Why did he keep staring at her as if she were a piece of molasses pie? And who was he, anyway? Did he know her? She blinked back tears. "You have me at a disadvantage, sir." He acted as if he knew her. She must have come by train to enlist the services of this man. But for what? What would have made her travel to Minnesota from…wherever she'd come from?

He edged closer, encircling her elbow and leaning in. "Why don't we sit down and talk?"

She needed a bath, warm and soapy, to ease away the frustrations and confusion filling her head—her heart. If she could relax, she might remember who she was. This man, good-looking though he was, merely presented another obstacle.

She drew her arm away. "Mr. Callahan, talking will do me no good. I am tired and dirty."

His face showed obvious compassion. His eyes targeted hers as surely as a dart. Did she play darts? Did her father, a man friend, a brother? The crooked smile on Mr. Callahan's lips offered its own kind of sympathy. She stood to his chin. He wasn't tall, wasn't short. His wide shoulders and slim waist caused her to stare a minute longer than proper before determining he appeared just right. Like the muscular build on one of the bulls in neighbor Spencer's field.

Neighbor Spencer? She had a neighbor named Spencer? Surely, if she could remember a neighbor, she'd soon recall her own name.

His hand nudged her arm. Not to be manhandled again, she jerked back.

"Mr. Callahan, the railroad is putting us up in the hotel across the street. Tomorrow, I intend to speak with a doctor." She'd speak with anyone at all to discover who she was. "If you'll excuse me." She took a shaky step but stopped soon enough.

"Rebecca. I'm here because we're supposed to be married tomorrow."

Her hand covered her heart. "Married?" Head whirling, her eyes fluttered and her legs turned to jelly as he grabbed her to him.

## Chapter 2

Fingers clutching, Jared supported Rebecca from falling to the ground. Picking her up easily, he strode immediately to the hotel down the road and across the street, dust and pebbles scuffing under his boots.

He stared into the beautiful face against his shoulder. More beautiful than he'd hoped, she was also light as a breeze and fit well in his arms. Perfect for his wife.

His wife. The words tripped through his thoughts so easily. If all went according to plan, he would find a way for them to be married tomorrow. He took in every bit of her face from her sooty lashes to her heart-shaped mouth.

When they arrived at the front of the hotel, Jared shouted for assistance. "Ben, can you help me out here?"

The withered hotel manager, Ben Sherwood, loped through the crowd in the doorway. "I got some hardcash customers in there. What's all the racket?" He stopped short. "Oh my. Poor little thing. This the girl you been waiting on?"

"She is, but she took a hit to the head during the train wreck. Doc Parker in there checking on folks?"

Ben glanced over his shoulder, indicating the back of the building. "Yeah. Got a makeshift hospital in the mudroom. Why don't you take her right on through?"

Marching across the lobby with his arms full, Jared stifled a sneeze at the sudden antiseptic odor tickling his nose. He stopped outside the door and waited. "Doc? This lady here's Rebecca Layne. She just fainted away in my arms."

Doc Parker's gaze bore a mischievous wink when he waved them in. "Well, you are the ladies' man, now, aren't you, Jared?"

Jared pushed the annoyance into his belly. "Listen, she's hurt and needs your help. Can't you see that bump on her head? And there's blood on her glove. Looks like she cut her hand."

The doctor pushed the spectacles from his nose up to his eyes and took a closer look. "Yessir, that's a bump, all right." He shoved a portly gent with nothing except a bruised ego to the side. "Let's get her on up here and we'll see what we'll see."

Jared laid her reverently on the table and the doc wagged a small bottle under her nose. She bolted upright, eyes wide and frightened.

"What are you doing?" Her face showed instant displeasure at being prodded and poked, but the doctor eased her back onto the makeshift examination table.

"There, now, miss. You've been hurt."

"I guess I know that."

"Well, feisty, that's a good sign. Jared, no reason you can't find the justice of the peace in a few days and get married like you planned."

This time, Rebecca sat up straight, yanked the doctor's hand away from her and aimed her wrath at Jared. "What is this constant nonsense about my marrying you? I have no intention of marrying anyone." She fought to drop her legs over the side, pushing the doc's hands away from her.

Jared cleared his throat. "Rebecca, we planned this."

"I didn't plan a thing, and, Mr. Callahan, stop calling me Rebecca!"

Doc smirked and helped her down. "Your injuries probably appear worse than they are. Always plenty of blood around the head, but there's not much we can do about head injuries except to watch them. You should recover in a few days. I think you can safely go now. Keep this bandage on your hand. There might be more swelling tonight. Watch for red around the cut. Bathe it in warm, soapy water two more times tonight. If it's redder in the morning, come back by and I'll have another check of the wound." He looked to Jared with a jerk of his head. "Have the hotel keep watch on her a couple times tonight. Head injury and all."

Jared reached out, but she swatted him away. His scowl spoke before his words. "Listen, Rebecca. If you'd let me talk to you for a few minutes, I might be able to clear this all up."

She'd be the one to clear things up. She wasn't going to marry anyone, even if the entire town banded against her with hot tar and feathers. Rebecca Layne, indeed.

And what was all this about marrying some cowhand or pig farmer or whatever he was?

His face pleaded with her. He must know her somehow. No man would march into a situation like this and try to walk off with a stranger. Would he?

"How about if we just sit in Millie's Restaurant across the street and talk? I'll buy you dinner. You must be hungry by now."

Her stomach rumbled. "I'll buy my own dinner." She reached for her bag, but her fingers met nothing except air. No purse, no overnight bag, not even a handkerchief to call her own. Her stomach growled again, deciding for her. "Well, if you insist. I'll speak with you for a few minutes. No harm in that. Which way is the restaurant?"

After the delicious roast chicken, biscuits with honey and fresh apple pie, her attitude improved significantly. She even found it agreeable to smile at him and thank him for the meal. "I am sorry if I sounded so harsh earlier. This has not been the best trip thus far."

Mr. Callahan pulled a paper from his pocket. "Here, maybe if you read this, it will help you to remember. Believe me, I'm not one to go about expecting unfamiliar young ladies to marry me."

Why he would need a mail-order bride was beyond her. His looks alone should be able to melt any heart in town. Maybe there was a shortage of eligible women. Maybe there were things about this man she couldn't imagine in her worst thoughts. She snapped back.

"It won't bite you."

*But you might.* She chewed the edge of her lip and accepted the letter with her good hand. She sniffed the lilac scent. Lilac, one of her favorites. Yes! She remembered—it *was* one of her favorite scents!

She eyed him, waiting for him to behave in an untoward manner. He smiled at her and nodded. "Go ahead."

*August 21, 1882*
*Dearest Jared,*
*The time is almost here. I have to laugh to think that just four months ago I answered an ad in the paper for a mail-order bride. My sister is still so scandalized she hardly speaks to me. But I simply could not allow my family to marry me off to the highest bidder like a mare ready to foal. Pardon my immodesty on this topic.*

*These past months, writing to you, have convinced me I want to live in the West. I hope you are as anxious as I for our marriage. Your darling little house sounds like heaven to me and I cannot wait to get to Worthville.*

*I'll be arriving at eleven on the morning of September tenth. I hope you'll be anxiously awaiting my train.*
*Yours lovingly, Rebecca Layne*

Did the words sound like her? She didn't know.
*Yours lovingly...*
She stared at the signature. Flowery. Definitely a woman's handwriting. She wouldn't know for sure if it was hers until her hand healed and she had cause to sign a letter or document. What a calamitous mess. If she *was* Rebecca Layne, no wonder she had run away. Her family sounded simply horrid. Of course, she didn't have the slightest idea who her family was and how peculiar they might be. She closed her eyes and sighed. She had to face facts—she might have written the letter.

No. Not possible. She would surely remember planning her own wedding.

"I'm certain I have never seen this before. I could tell if I had composed such a…personal letter. If you will excuse me now, I'm tired and must be shown my room. I have to soak this wound." She held out her left hand. "Nice to have met you, Mr. Callahan. Thank you for dinner. And I hope you find the lady for whom you are searching. But that lady is most assuredly not me."

As she stood to leave, a booming voice filtered across the room. "There you are. Have you seen a doctor, young lady?"

"Mr. Fletcher?" The man who'd helped her. She dropped her gaze. He was also the man who'd made her so uncomfortable. And here she stood, trapped between the proverbial rock and a hard place. Who could she trust?

Callahan jumped from his seat before Mr. Fletcher could answer. He pushed ahead of her and planted his legs shoulder width apart, practically daring the man to move her direction. He glanced over his shoulder. "Is this fellow bothering you, Rebecca?"

"No. *You* are bothering me, if truth be told. Now, if you'll excuse me." And she flitted around him, reaching for Fletcher's outstretched arm.

Once outside, she dropped his grasp as quickly as possible and stalked across the street toward the hotel. No one would be telling her what to do or where to go until she could figure out who she was. And then she would decide.

Mr. Fletcher tipped his hat and smiled. "Perhaps we'll meet again, dear lady. Get some rest and take care of yourself. But if you find you need anything at all, be my guest. I will be your obedient servant."

Humph. She was pretty sure she would never accept the assistance of a smarmy man like Mr. Fletcher.

Entering the lobby of the modest establishment, she gazed about, taking in the other passengers and wondered if the hotel would have enough room. From the outside, it appeared to be huge, but inside was another story. The counter ran less than an arm's length and the stairs to the right wound steeply to the first floor. How many rooms were there at the top?

Her fears were put to rest when the hotel keep placed a key on the counter. He opened the large leather register and pointed to her. "Sign here, please. The railroad will pay, but you must sign in so they'll see you stayed here."

When he asked her to sign her name, she hesitated. Perhaps she *should* sign Rebecca Layne. What other choice did she have if she couldn't remember her real name? Was it possible she had come here alone to marry a stranger? Was she that kind of girl—a girl who would leave her family to meet a man she didn't know? Why not? He wasn't the only unknown to her; she, too, was a stranger to herself.

A man pushed her from behind without apology. "Any more rooms?"

Afraid she might lose the one she had, she pulled her injured hand from her side, supported it with her left and as neatly as possible signed: Rebecca Layne.

Jared stripped the last creamy drops from Star's udders, but the calf continued to push in, competing for the milk. He laughed and rubbed the marking on her forehead: a star, just like her ma's. "Move back, girl. There's plenty for both of us."

He slid his palm down to her nose, rubbing the velvety softness. "Enough now. You have your own pail of milk. Let's not be selfish." He smiled at the quivering legs that were growing steadier every day.

With the two new calves, the three from last year, their mas and his bull, Jared saw his small herd growing. Soon he'd be able to wean the runt, Dauber, as well, which would mean even more milk. And more milking. A frown started but he immediately tamped it down. No sense whining about too much work. His part-time help and the woman he had thought he would marry would have been more than enough, but now he was spread too thin.

After breakfast, he intended to return the three miles to town in spite of how tired Charger must be. He wasn't a workhorse, but with Tinker still sore, Charger had been the one to pull the wagon to town to meet Rebecca's train. And he'd been less than happy standing around all day in the hot sun. Now his favorite mount would have to endure the circuit a second time in two days. Jared only hoped Rebecca had come to her senses and remembered who she was and why she was here. He didn't have time to be chasing a woman around. After all, wasn't that why he'd sent for her in the first place? No time for courting one of the snooty town women who made it obvious they liked the fact that his ranch prospered. Whenever he entered town for supplies or church, women sought him out. Well, no, thank you very much. He preferred a woman who didn't have a grasp of his ranch's worth. And he wasn't good at talking with women.

Rebecca wanted a country life. At least, that's what she'd said in her letters. And he needed a wife. Taking care of the ranch animals, the chickens and a small garden, and then baching it, left him more than a little tired. Plus, and he hated to admit this, he wanted a woman to share his life with, to raise more than chickens and cows; he wanted to raise a family, give some meaning to what God intended a life to be.

From her letters, he'd thought Rebecca had wanted the same things. He hadn't told her how well the ranch was doing. Instead, he hoped for a woman who wanted him for himself, not his money. And he had thought that was what he was getting. Now he wasn't sure.

Jared grabbed the buckets of milk and lugged them into the house. He strained the milk, hauled the pans down to the cellar and left the thick cream to cool. Once upstairs again, he started breakfast. Setting bacon to fry, he picked out the largest eggs from the bowl on the counter. Then he added more milk, a pinch of sugar and flour to the sourdough mix until he had a thick, sweet batter for fried cakes.

Thanking God every day he'd learned to cook from his sister, Olivia, he poured the batter and smelled the strong coffee boiling. His stomach rumbled in anticipation of melted butter and brown sugar dripping over the sides of the hotcakes.

She chewed the edge of her lip, afraid to ask. But sitting straighter, she locked eyes with the waiter. "You are sure the railroad is paying for our food? All of it?"

"Yes, miss. All of it. For the next week, until they can clear the pass and send a new train, you folks are guests of the Pacific Railway. We'll do our best to make you right at home."

"But there are so many of us."

He smiled. "Not as many as you'd think. Most of those folks on the train were headed here anyway. Only a few moving on. So don't you worry your pretty little head."

She stared again at the food-bespeckled sheet of brown paper that served as the restaurant menu. "I'll have two eggs and toast and jam with a dish of fried apples and onions, please." As he started to walk away, she blurted, "And tea, with lots and lots of cream and sugar."

*She must like tea. With plenty of cream and sugar.* That was good to know. Or at least it was a start.

Her hand tensed around the steel fork. Her fingers felt stronger, less painful today. Very little redness around the cut. She might try using her right hand more often and see how well she did. Would that farmer show up as he said he would? How dreadful not to know anything about him. While she was daydreaming, the door opened. She looked up, expecting—she wasn't sure who.

Without fanfare, the stationmaster entered and cleared his throat. "Folks, thought I'd catch most of you having breakfast." He lifted a paper from his side. "This here's what the railroad has planned for you. At the end of the week, anyone who wants to return home will be taken back by way of Chicago, just like you came. Anyone looking to go on will also be allowed to travel without cost to them. But anyone choosing to stay is on their own. They're sorry for all the inconvenience, but these things happen. Anyone planning to fix their sights here just needs to let me know and you'll still be put up for the week. After that, your arrangements will be on you. Are there any questions?"

She swallowed hard and lifted a forkful of tender eggs while folks chattered about the railroad's assistance. She didn't know where home even was. If she went back, would she have a home to go to? If she went on ahead, the same unknown fate would await her. If she stayed, she would have to find work. At least she understood she was supposed to be acquainted with someone here. This was as a good a place as any to put down stakes, at least until her memory returned. Jam-slathered toast waited for her on an otherwise nearly empty plate.

The stationmaster finished explaining how they should sign for each meal as she took the last bite of tender apple. She washed it down with plenty of tea.

No matter what, if she were to stay she would have to locate work. No respectable woman would even think of marrying a stranger.

She finished the last drops in the cup and rose.

Across the street at the hotel, she spoke softly to the old gent behind the counter. "Do you know of anyone hiring in town?"

"What do you do, Miss Layne?"

"I—uh. Well, I'm not sure. I think I can cook. Probably sew." She tapped her finger on her chin. "That's it. I can sew. I can see the fabric running through my fingers. Is there a seamstress in town in need of help?"

"Well. You go across the street, four buildings down. There's a general store, post office and Miss Beadie keeps a small corner where she makes shirts and the like for the shopkeeper. Can't say as I've heard of her doing much about ladies' things, but you could ask, Miss Layne. You understand, most ladies around here do their own dressmaking."

"Yes. Thank you. I will."

She stared as her fingers tapped a nervous rhythm on her other arm. *Gracious, do I sew well enough to work for someone else?*

Entering the store, she searched over the barrels of food and bolts of fabric to the back. In the corner, stitching like a house afire, an older woman revved her treadle sewing machine until the fabric fairly flew off the front. Rebecca stopped and stared.

Over the clacking she said, "Miss Beadie? I'm Rebecca Layne and I heard you might need an extra hand on these shirts?"

"Lands, child." Miss Beadie stopped and placed a hand on her hip. "I barely earn enough to keep a soul in flour and coffee. And I'll be honest with you, you don't look like you're in any condition to be sewing."

Her hand throbbed and she nodded.

"But if you'd like to write down your name and where to get hold of you, I'll let you know if business becomes too much for one woman. Miss Layne, did ya say?"

*Miss Layne.* She nodded and signed the name on a pattern cover and then left the store. On the way out, she eyed the red apples in one of the bins. A crisp apple sounded like heaven to her, but without money, she had to make do with the meals the railroad provided. If only the seamstress had needed help.

The sun had already heated up the outdoors. Bees hovered over the fruit barrels in the front, tasting of the luscious juice. She'd love to taste it, as well. As wonderful as the apples and pears looked, though, she could never be tempted enough to help herself. She wasn't raised that way; of that much, she was sure.

She licked her lips and glanced up. The farmer reappeared at her side. He chose the ripest apple and tossed it her direction. "Let me pay for this and I'll meet you at the hotel."

"But—"

"No buts, Rebecca. I'm glad to do it. Just give me a minute to go inside."

She smelled the apple and her hunger pangs caused her to smile. "Thank you, but you won't be meeting me anywhere, Mr. Callahan. I'll owe you for the apple."

*My, what a stubborn woman.* Did he really want that quality in a wife? He must be desperate as an old bull in a field without cows to consider marrying her.

Her footsteps stirred up dust in the street. Even as she walked away, it was obvious she was a fine figure of a woman. He groaned. He'd resorted to thinking of her as a fine figure when, in fact, their plans had been for her to be his bride.

Perhaps she was no different, after all, from the many women in town who had sought out his company. In church, in the stores, they stared, they whispered. One daring young lady even called him by his given name. The boldness nowadays flustered him, and that had been one of the primary reasons he'd advertised for a bride.

When he glanced up from his daydreams, Rebecca had licked the apple juice from her lips and turned toward the hotel. The first thought that came to mind was to follow her like his pa's old dog, Cherokee. He'd chased every stray female in the county but never seemed to make any headway. Well, he'd be dog tied if he'd traipse after Rebecca the same way. He'd had his say, shown her who he was and now it was up to her whether or not they continued with their plans.

The town beauty, Clacinda—Clancy—Sherwood, daughter of the hotel keep, strolled in front of Rebecca. Taller by about three inches and much slimmer, Clancy shook her head full of chestnut hair and bumped against Rebecca. He saw her mouth an apology but she quickly glanced across the street at Jared. She waved a gloved hand. He couldn't help noticing Rebecca's reaction. Her face glowed red, her eyes narrowed and that pleasing figure tensed. She showed her back to Clancy and to him, strolling into the hotel with head held high.

Jared's good intentions took flight. Like it or not, Rebecca had become a challenge, and he'd never been one to let a challenge go. Or was it the way her eyes flashed her every feeling right out into the open that caused him to long for the chase?

With a groan, he wiped sweaty palms on his pants and veered around a pouting Clancy.

"Jared? Can't you say hello on such a beautiful day?"

He tipped his hat. "Afternoon, Miss Sherwood." When she moved toward him, he continued on his way, straight to the hotel, leaving Clancy in the dust like a swatted hornet. And if he read her correctly, just as angry.

## *Chapter 3*

Later that day after she'd refused to come downstairs again, she had indulged herself in a case of the miseries. What was going to become of her? She had no money, no prospects for work, nowhere to live. Soon, her life would look less rosy than today. And each day in the town was worse than the last. Three days ago had spelled the beginning of her gloom.

A chance meeting with Mr. Fletcher in Millie's, when he'd smiled and asked to sit with her, helped her make a decision. Lunch was followed by everyday conversation that eventually drifted to Mr. Fletcher's offering to assist her in finding work.

She hung her head, resigned to doing any menial task. "The only job I've heard about is the saloon. They need another female to do whatever females do in saloons." Her face warmed as she thought about all that might entail. She probably shouldn't have mentioned it.

Fletcher patted her hand when he spoke. "I suppose it's nothing more than being a pretty waitress, like Millie. But it's no place for a lady." His eyes raked her head to toe and he left her feeling as if she'd been stripped to her shimmy shirt.

She drew her now-shaking hand back. "You're probably right."

She got to her feet, needing to get away from this man who seemed helpful and yet caused her stomach to churn with worry. She had to admit, even with reservations, that farmer didn't cause her any worry like this man, not yet, anyway.

His gaze followed her. She stopped at the door, shaking, then hurried from the restaurant to her only refuge—the hotel.

Here she had stayed holed up for three days, only coming out for her meals.

And last night, sleep had come at a premium, nightmares a constant reminder of what she'd lived through. But even in her dreams she wasn't able to discover her identity.

In her dream, a burning odor filled the air. She staggered, her feet as unsure as her swirling head. She gagged into her hankie.

A quick glance at the smoking debris surrounding her answered none of her questions. Heat shivered off the ground, extending toward her from the train like rippling fingers of fire. People screamed; an old woman, sitting atop a smashed leather case, sobbed into a glove. Others wandered about in a daze. They stumbled as if in a vacuum, dizzily ambling through the motions.

A loud *pop!* A snap—hundreds of snaps—and then a deafening crunch.

Through the sting of smoke-filled eyes, she watched as the steam engine heaved and groaned onto its side. Flames licked at what was left of the smoldering frame. Chunks separated in a frightening metallic screech and crashed to the ground.

In seconds, bits and pieces of luggage and ash scattered farther with each gust of air.

"Miss, are you all right?" A gentleman hovered as if she might fall. At last, he held out his hand.

"Who are you?"

His forehead drew into a frown. "I'm a gentleman here to help. Can I get you something? Do you have a traveling companion with you?"

"I'm…I—uh. I don't know. I'm not sure." In her hand she held a monogrammed hankie. She lifted tender fingers to her head. Pain ricocheted from one side to the other and a huge lump rose under her bruised palm. When she pulled her hand away, blood dampened her glove. From her head or her fingers? Her glove, slit across the side, exposed a cut that ran deep. "I seem to be hurt."

"Let's sit you down and get a cold cloth for that bump if I can find one. The name's Gordon Fletcher." He shoved a big paw in her direction. A gold ring on each hand hinted at… What?

"And I'm…my name's… I'll stay right here and wait for you." Feeling around for her purse, she found only soil and tufts of grass. The hankie fluttered from her hand and blew across the scorched prairie, out of reach.

He turned his back. "There's a lady here needs help!"

"Really, I'm fine." She wasn't fine. She didn't know

her name. Didn't know where she was. Her stomach lurched.

Mr. Fletcher turned back around and removed his coat. He draped the heavy wool on the ground and offered her a smile, but not a friendly, helpful type of smile. She didn't like the way his lips pursed into it or the way his eyes slithered over her. "You sit down. I'll see if there is a doctor among the passengers."

Fletcher left, his hand tight around the handle of a small reticule.

She lifted her hand to her head again, fighting the urge to scream and run. But where would she go? Her destination? Oh, she wasn't sure of anything. And why was that?

The goose egg, of course. Her aching fingers skimmed over the source of the splintering pain behind her eyes as another loud crash caught her off guard. One of the cars separated from the rest and rolled down the incline like a boulder down a hill. She sucked back a gasp, and with it came soot and hot air that parched her throat.

She eyed a large canvas bag tumbling behind the train, burn spots dotting the edges. Could that be her bag? But then a few envelopes escaped the open edge and blew around in circles. A mailbag. She trembled in spite of the heat and hugged her arms around her. Where had that man gone? She didn't see him anymore.

The sound of someone hammering outside awakened her at last. Dazed from her dream, she was surprised she wasn't able to smell smoke and that all was quiet around her. She remembered what had happened on the train now, but the dream had brought her no nearer to knowing who she was.

She brushed the sleep from her eyes and checked

carefully out the window to be sure there was no sign of that Mr. Fletcher or the farmer who wanted her to marry him. She didn't need either of them adding to her distress.

After splashing water on her face, she took another peek and spied Jared in the distance. Talking with him, seeing his ranch, was the furthest desire from her heart. Though she tried to convince herself he was the last man she would ever consider marrying, she pictured the coffee-brown eyes that had smiled at her when they had first met. The kind of eyes that sent a girl's heart fluttering in her chest. Expressive, compassionate eyes.

Oh, who was she kidding? She thought of no one but Jared Callahan. That was why she peeked out the window, hoping he was waiting for her. And yet she hadn't given him a moment's notice. Each day he rode into town, stood downstairs, sent a note requesting her company and left when she refused to come down. She flopped across the bed. This tiny room, no bigger than a closet, was hers for two more days. She probably had a beautiful room at home, only she didn't know where home was or whether she still had a home. And before long she would have to make living arrangements, and that meant finding a job.

Suddenly the odor in the room overpowered her. She needed to buy new clothes, take a long, hot bath and figure out what she was going to do. The stuffiness pressed in on her. Life with Mr. Callahan couldn't be worse than this—or could it?

She took the stairs as fast as a man so she could at least talk to the farmer. And there he was, in his usual place. But before she could catch his attention, he mounted his horse and trotted toward the blacksmith's.

He hadn't even brought the buckboard this time. She'd no doubt convinced him at last that she meant business about not marrying him. And she was surprised that it bothered her so much. Maybe the wide shoulders that looked as if they could carry the worries of the world, or the deep-set brown eyes, had convinced her he cared a bit more than she liked.

Here she stood, hiding from the world so no man could bother her, but in time she would have to face facts. She didn't know where to go or who to go with. Hunger pangs twanged at her belly, but food didn't interest her. She returned to her room, her legs like heavy limbs.

As she removed her tattered gloves, a soft rap sounded at her door. "Miss Layne? You have a letter. Would you like me to slide it under your door? Miss Layne?"

She recognized the voice of Aggy, the maid. "Thank you, Aggy. That will be fine." There was no reason to read another of his letters. She had apparently read and responded to plenty of them already. But what if family had inquired of her? What if a letter from her mother, father, a husband… Oh, gracious! She should read the note immediately.

She slipped from the edge of the bed and stooped to retrieve the letter.

*My dearest Rebecca,*
*I can't begin to understand how afraid you must be having forgotten who I am. Who you are, for that matter. Be assured of one thing, I won't bother you anymore if you choose not to come to*

*me, but I have every reason to believe you and I
would have as reasonable a life together as any
other couple. Please meet me for dinner at one if
you would like me to take you to my ranch so you
can see it and make your decision. If you don't
come to Millie's, I will also understand and allow
you the privacy you seem to want.
Yours, Jared Callahan*

He *was* still in town. She had two more days to stay
in the hotel. After deciding not to go on and not to return to who knew where, she must determine whether
or not to become Jared Callahan's wife. And in short
order. Two days would pass very quickly, and after that
an empty belly loomed ahead.

With no father or brother to protect her, she had little to offer herself other than marrying the farmer. He
seemed decent enough. Probably had some shanty in
the middle of the prairie with a cow and a pig for her
to milk and slop. She didn't know, but she was sure she
hadn't slopped pigs before. Even without evidence of
her past, she realized that was not what she intended for
her future. And yet what other choice was there? Her
skirt and blouse, the same ones she'd been in for five
days, clung to her sweaty skin like barnacles on a ship.
She wouldn't have to be a lady of means to know she
needed a bath, new clothes and perhaps even a whiff
of lilac or lemon verbena scent to make her presentable once again.

She remembered Fletcher's odd expression when he'd
patted her hand, and she shuddered. Which was worse?
A life slopping drunken pigs in a saloon or slopping

hogs on a farm? No, Fletcher had been right about that, at least; the saloon was no place for a lady. That she was a lady, she had no doubt.

Jared sat in Millie's, a cup of good, strong coffee in his hands. He glanced up each time the door opened, but no Rebecca. At ten past one, he figured he'd give her one more minute before ordering dinner and a piece of Millie's delicious chocolate cake. He eyed a big wedge being served to the man at the next table and his mouth watered.

A shadow crossed the table. "Hey, Jared."

"Hey, to you, Ketch."

A man in his late fifties, Duncan Ketch drew a chair out and sat down. "You expecting company? If not, I thought I'd jaw a spell about those cattle getting lost in the lone rock area."

"I have a guest coming, but stop by the house this week and we'll see if we can figure out how to keep 'em away from the edge. I lost a foal this spring. How she got out I'll never know, but animals seem to be drawn to that place."

Duncan nodded and replaced the chair, but his eyes stayed glued to the empty seat next to Jared. When Jared didn't move to offer the place, Ketch headed toward the back.

Miss Millie walked past and Jared caught her attention. "Guess I'll order now."

"Your guest not coming?"

"Doesn't look like it. How about roasted chicken, a few corn dodgers or biscuits and a chunk of your chocolate cake?"

"Coming right up, good lookin'. And I'll be right by with more coffee." She winked.

He grinned and understood Millie was only being friendly. She flirted with all the customers; the wives didn't even take offense.

The door opened again and a hot breath of air blew into the room, accompanied by dusty whorls of leaves. Rebecca stood in the doorway, surveying the room with a vulnerability that tugged at his heart.

With a wave of his hand, he stood and invited her over.

"I didn't think you were going to come." But he'd hoped she would. One look at those innocent eyes would make a man hope all sorts of things, but he shook his head. He would just show her some kindness. Let her know that he cared. And he did care.

"I decided but a few minutes ago." She twisted her hands together as he pulled out her chair. "Thank you." She smiled. "You don't have a farmer's manners."

He narrowed his eyes. "Farmers aren't supposed to have manners?" She might look vulnerable but her behavior said otherwise. Farmers, indeed. He hadn't taken her for a snob.

She ignored his question with a blush and wrinkled her nose. "Tell me about yourself, Mr. Callahan." She settled into her seat and struggled over the small talk. "Apparently I don't remember much about myself." He thought he noticed moisture at the edges of her eyes.

She'd softened a might, and he wondered if she was here to give in and marry him. Out of desperation? Likely.

"Well, let's see. I was educated in the East, but all I wanted was to go West. Have a modest ranch I'm proud of. Building it from scratch eight years ago took some gumption, but I guess I had more of that at twenty-one than common sense. Right now it isn't all that much, but it's presentable. I have a few head of cattle and a string of good horses. Raise a couple of pigs for food."

"Pigs?"

"For food." What? Did she think he was a pig farmer now? "Nothing to write back home about yet, but I have hope my place will do well in time. I have several acres put to hay as feed for the animals, and a modest garden. Very small, actually. Some fruit trees. That's about it."

She glanced down at her hands. "I've thought over your offer." She looked up and her cheeks lost the battle, turned red as a bee sting. "I'll be honest. I don't know where my home is. I don't have any idea who I might be, other than what you have told me."

Her expression seemed to look into the unknown and return empty. Obviously she felt she had no other choice than to marry the "pig" farmer. His stomach clenched. "I'm sorry I don't know more to tell you. I have only the letters to go by."

"There's no work in town. And I haven't any offers that will allow me to take care of myself. If I am Rebecca Layne, then we presumably had an arrangement."

She had the resigned look of one who would rather face a firing squad than be forced into this marriage. "And life with me would be better than living on the streets?"

"I'm sorry. I didn't mean to put my feelings so rudely. But telling you I was interested in a husband… Well, I'm afraid you would see right through me."

His stomach knotted again at her words. He did prefer honesty over all else, but his self-confidence was taking a beating at the moment and it was difficult to feel very romantic. "So, you want to go ahead?"

She blinked those gorgeous blue eyes, pulling him in a little deeper, but for a moment only. Then reality returned. She wanted a home, clothes on her back and food in her belly. Nothing more.

A large crash sounded outside. Rebecca started.

Jared rose to the window, the woman right behind him.

One of the saloon girls had been thrown through a window of the Last Chance and lay like a broken doll on the ground. A gasp issued from Rebecca's lips.

"So that is how the West treats a lady?"

"That's how the saloon treats a lady, though she's not exactly known for being a lady. But I'd never say that to the poor woman. She has just as much right to be treated well as the next female." He stared at the scene unfolding. "More, perhaps. She's a kind soul. Only one there I'd trust turning my back to."

"You go there often?"

"Not so anyone would notice." He cocked his head to the side. "I'm not a drinking man, if that's what you're asking."

He choked back what he'd wanted to say as a burly man from the saloon pulled the girl, Jesse, back through the door, her arm twisting at a bad angle. "And no, that's not how women are treated out here. She was probably in the wrong place at the wrong time. Most of those girls would rather be in another life, but they don't have any other experience. Or someone brought them out here and died. They all have a story to tell." Just then, a man flew out the same window and lay where Jesse had been.

Rebecca's lip trembled. "I'm not sure the West is all I imagined it would be. If I could remember what I imagined, that is."

"If I've heard that once, I've heard it a thousand times. Folks come thinking this will solve all their problems only to find themselves with new problems."

Her hand tried to cover a quivering lip.

"Well, what's your decision?"

She glanced around, a blank expression on her face. "My what?"

"About the marriage, I mean." If he were truthful with himself, he'd fallen for her just a bit in the letters and even more since she'd arrived. Stubborn and irascible as she was, a spark shone from her depths—a spark that might flame one day if he stayed patient and kind.

She licked her lips, those alluring eyes straining back toward the window as he and Rebecca took their seats again. "All right, I'll live up to my part of the bargain if you still want me." Now, instead of trembling, her chin jutted forward, daring him to accept her as she was.

Fighting the urge to smile outright, afraid he'd frighten her off with his enthusiasm, instead, he reached across the table and enclosed her hand in his. "I'd like that."

Through the stoic veneer, a tear dribbled from her eye and she hesitated before drawing her hand from his to dab the moisture away, but he beat her to it with a hankie he'd withdrawn from his pocket. "Then our agreement is settled." She nodded as her gaze dropped to the table.

Would he enjoy a normal married life or would she forever be a stranger? "Rebecca, I can't make you any promises."

She lifted her napkin to her lips as if she could hide behind it. "I understand."

With no more talk, they finished their meal with some of Millie's cake and Jared walked her from the busy restaurant to the general store. He asked Miss Beadie to help Rebecca with necessities to tide her over until they could order new clothes from the catalog Beadie had on hand.

"I could try and sew a few if the yard goods aren't too dear," Rebecca offered.

"You sew?"

She hesitated. "I think so. I remember feeling fabric sliding through my fingers. I must sew. Perhaps I could try before you spend so much money ordering clothes for me. I don't feel right about you buying anything for me."

Miss Beadie eyed them suspiciously.

"You can't stay in that same dress forever, Rebecca. Let's be honest here. Even if you do sew, your hand is in no condition. I think we had better order from the catalog." He turned to Miss Beadie. "Do you suppose you could stitch up two women's dresses, one good and one work dress, for now? I know it's a lot to ask on such short notice."

"Certainly, Mr. Callahan. I'll have them finished end of the week."

"That soon?" Rebecca asked. "I'm ever so grateful, Miss Beadie."

Jared led her to the other side of the store where women's unmentionables were kept hidden from view. "You'd better get some fresh things. Whatever you need." Then he strolled out front to watch a boisterous checkers match.

* * *

Her face burned. *Fresh things.* Of course, she must be a sight. One half bath all week and the same dirty clothes. Only her personal items had been washed and dried overnight, but her skirt and blouse were sweaty, smudged and disorderly. What must he think of her?

After she finished picking out new undergarments, she bade Miss Beadie goodbye and walked out front. She sheltered her eyes from the sun and drank in the gray boards that covered the fronts of each building. Had they been painted once or just left to weather? She couldn't be sure. The saloon looked as if it might have had yellow milk paint on it once. And the hotel...

"Rebecca? You ready to go?" He reached for the bundles she carried.

"What? Oh yes."

Loaded with packages in one hand, Jared steered her toward a wagon with the other. "I hope you bought enough, Rebecca."

"It feels peculiar spending your money, Mr. Callahan."

"That *was* the idea."

The blush began again, in earnest, as the horse stomped its foot. Rebecca wanted to stomp hers, too. "Didn't you ride your horse to town this morning?"

He smirked at her around the bundles. "You *have* been paying attention. Maybe I'm not as distasteful as you originally thought?"

"I beg your pardon?"

His eyes sparkled with mischief. "You've been watching me ride into town."

She raised her hand to quiet him. "Do not say another word, Mr. Callahan, or I shan't go with you." She flamed with heat. He had obviously noticed her observing him from the window, but how could he be arrogant enough to mention her indiscretion?

Jared stopped, shifted the packages against his hip. "Rebecca, I was only teasing you. I do that a lot once I know someone, so you'd better accustom yourself to that. My sister and I played tricks on each other all the time as children. I don't suppose I'll change my ways at this point. Yes, I rode my horse into town, but I have had a buggy ready for hire anytime you might say yes. Charger can trot along behind. He's quite tired of pulling the wagon."

He hoisted the packages into the back of the buggy, then reached for her hand to help her in. She pulled away and stumbled, but Jared caught her elbow. They locked eyes and for a few blissful, confusing seconds, his grin sent shivers through her stomach.

"Are you all right?" he whispered.

She licked dry lips again before speaking. "Fine, thank you." Not fine at all. She could barely breathe. Had she ever felt this way before? Perhaps she had a husband back home and her stomach fluttered like this all the time, or he might have been an ogre, treated her horribly. *Oh my.* Maybe that was it and she had run away.

# Chapter 4

Charger balked hard against the back of the buggy, no doubt sensing the barn close at hand and looking forward to his feed. Jared stopped outside the barn and jumped from his seat. He untied his horse from the carriage. When he returned to help Rebecca down, she stared, her mouth a round O.

"This is hardly a prairie shanty."

"No. It most certainly is not. I'm sure I never mentioned a prairie shanty in any of my letters."

She raised the new hankie to her lips, wiping dust from her mouth. "But I thought—"

"Then, dear lady, you thought wrong." He helped her from the buggy, over the wheels and down to the ground. "Would you care for a tour?" His hand clasped her arm and guided her past the corral. Horses nickered and lifted their heads in his direction. He was sure his pride showed as he walked her around the barn and outbuildings.

"My, it's a large ranch. So many trees. It's really quite beautiful here. And the farmland stretches a good way. Why, you must have spent a great deal of time clearing the land."

Not able to read her expression, good or bad, Jared hoped the place would entice her to stay. But perhaps she wanted a small home to care for. He'd known women who didn't want such responsibility as this. Yet in her letters she said she longed to help with a ranch. Was she remembering that or had she completely forgotten all they'd discussed? Could he even be sure this woman was Rebecca Layne? Foolishness! Of course she was Rebecca. There had been no other young lady on the train, no other woman unaccounted for. Wasn't that what the stationmaster had told him?

He glanced at her from the corner of his eye. She had a habit of biting the edge of her lip. Did that mean she liked his spread or regretted her decision?

Once the grand tour was over, he sat with her on the porch swing, wasting time in idle chatter and the soft swaying of the swing. "There's something I'd like to say."

She faced him, fear instead of stubbornness on her face. "Oh?"

"Rebecca, you know how I feel. Now that you've had a chance to look the place over, I hope you will still say yes. If so, we'll go into town, see the justice of the peace and get ourselves married. If not, you keep these few things we bought and I'll pay for you to return home."

Her hands fluttered in her lap. "Home? I am afraid I'm not sure where that is, Mr. Callahan. Home. My, but it does sound good. Only I wouldn't be able to tell you where to send me." Her breath hitched audibly. Should he try to comfort her? "No. I made a decision to go through with your offer. Here I am. Here I plan to stay."

She wanted to be anywhere but here; he could tell. Why was he pressuring her to marry him when all she longed for was her family back home? Perhaps he should try and contact them. "You needn't worry, Rebecca. I'll drive you to town, buy you supper and we'll see about getting you a ticket home."

"But where would that be?"

"Don't be foolish, girl. We know your name and your address. I'm sure your family would be anxious for you to return to them if you're not happy here." He shifted in the seat, gazing directly into her eyes. Honesty was always the best policy. "As anxious as I am for you to stay."

She sat straighter, her back stiff and refined. "Mr. Callahan. From the sound of the letter you showed me, I do not have much of a happy family awaiting me." She turned her head away. "For whatever reason, I made these plans, and I intend to honor them. As long as you are willing to be…patient with me." Her shoulders shivered in spite of the heat. "Give me time to learn to know you again. After all, you have been kind up to now."

He understood exactly what she meant by his being patient. Would he be patient? Would they ever truly be man and wife? Here was his dream in one small, beautiful woman, but she didn't remember anything about him. Anything about their dreams together. He would have to wait. Until she was ready to be his wife, he planned to be a very patient man. He looked around and for one second wished he could punch something—anything. Drawing in a deep breath, he calmed himself.

Without any effort whatsoever, his hand came to rest over her fingers. "I promise to wait, Rebecca. Have no qualms about that." Would he merely be her provider and she a servant for his ranch? He did need the help, at any rate. Though he had hoped for a wife in every sense of…in time, perhaps. Honoring his promise, he drew back his hand.

Mr. Jared Callahan had made it clear, at least in her mind, that he was willing to accept her as nothing more than a servant in his home. Of course, he'd be patient. No need to be anything else with the hired help. He had all the time in the world to toss her an apron and a wooden spoon and steer her toward the kitchen. But what choice did she have? If she were Rebecca Layne, her family sounded absolutely horrid. She wouldn't want to return to them. No. This was her only solution to a grave problem that started when the train ran off the tracks and she was transported to the small town of Worthville, miles from civilization.

Jared headed to the barn, so she sat on the porch swing and thought about the accident.

As the noon sun had lost its unbearable reach that day, sliding behind thick clouds, the folks whose lives had been spared gathered together. Some prayed and others shared what meager food they had discovered in their satchels.

"Here you go, young lady." A woman bedecked in feathers and lace offered a slice of bread with a thin smear of butter. Then she riffled through her bag and pulled out a piece of cloth. "Here, wrap your fingers real tight now so they don't swell."

"Thank you. Does anyone know where we are?" The food tasted dry and she could hardly choke down two bites of the dark, stale bread.

The woman sniffed. "I heard the man in charge say we're about twenty miles west of Rochester, Minnesota. Lands, how did this happen? Trains don't simply jump off the tracks." The outlandish woman huffed a couple of minutes more and then left.

Ongoing waves of heat spread over the prairie, blanket after blanket of scorching air. Shifting for a comfortable position, she felt blood ooze down the side of her face, cooling her cheek for a second.

Afternoon brought little relief. She gazed about her, engaging in conversation every now and then with strangers, but all she hoped for was a glimpse into her life, a vignette of where she'd come from and where she might be traveling. Maybe if she found the monogrammed hankie it would give her a clue to at least her name.

Before she could search for it, wagons appeared over the ridge, wheels clattering, dust rising. As they drew closer, she observed horses wheezing against the whip. Five teams in all struggled to drag the huge wagons over the rutted and bumpy prairie. The horses shied from the heat of the fire.

She rose to her feet for a better look, ignoring the jacket lying in the dirt.

Finally, an old man, well fed but nimble, dropped to the ground from the lead wagon, shaded his eyes and mumbled to one of the men in the group. "Can't take you back to Rochester. We were told to haul all of you to the next station. Worthville. About ten miles from here. There'll be another train once we clear this here track. Then you folks can go on about yer business to wherever you're headed. Let's load 'em up." He directed his attention to the ladies first, in a fatherly manner.

She offered her hand to the man, winced and stepped into a wagon bed full of straw. The feathered woman and skinny man slouched next to her. Others leaned against the rough-hewn sides and closed their eyes, probably hoping for answers, as she did. Only, they knew what questions to ask.

She shifted around a sharp splinter of wood.

The man she presumed to be the boss leaned an arm against the slat behind her back. "You folks hang on tight. We wanna see to it you get into town before sunset."

A last look over her shoulder exposed the outright chaos of her day. And to think, *she* was one of the lucky ones.

Well, she couldn't dwell on the horrible day that had changed her life. She had to face this day and make a decision. While Jared was in the barn caring for his cows, she went into the kitchen and strolled about, investigating every corner and nook. Through the back of the kitchen, there was a long, well-stocked pantry, adjacent to the main room. White cupboards and drawers lined the connecting wall and were filled with every imaginable necessity. It would be a joy to prepare meals here. It was not exactly being tossed a wooden spoon, as she had first imagined. He kept a clean house for a man and apparently enjoyed some of the good things in life. Not exactly her idea of a pig farmer, anymore.

She stepped to the pantry window and gazed out.

Jared must still be in the barn, as the door was open. There must be a great deal of livestock for such a big barn. And smaller outbuildings sat west of the barn. A woodshed, perhaps? She giggled, suddenly remembering having her britches dusted as a child in the woodshed. Oh, why couldn't she remember more than a spanking?

When she finished surveying the kitchen, her footsteps fell in the direction of the bedroom. One large room, masculine looking with a big window, faced the back and overlooked a well-kept garden. Barbed wire surrounded all the vegetables, no doubt to keep out deer and other wild creatures. She touched the edge of the bed. Soft. But she wouldn't be expected to stay in here with a stranger, would she?

On closer inspection, she found another, smaller room at the front of the house. This room must be a guest room, or the room intended one day for a baby.

Her cheeks blazed hot like a fire.

A small bed with a cream-colored quilt perched along one side. Her imagination took over. Perhaps his mother had made the quilt. This room could be for guests. For lady friends? Surely not! Though she had to admit he was a very handsome man. Remembering the redhead in town, she wondered if the woman had ever slept beneath the creamy quilt.

She put her hands on her face and felt the heat once again. Shame on her to let that cross her mind. Lately, all she had to do was think about him and warmth covered her cheeks. Why had she ever agreed to stay? What would life be like with a total stranger by her side? A man whose personal life she knew nothing about?

\* \* \*

The ride into town stirred little but dust on the road. For the longest time, they didn't exchange a single word; she simply watched the back end of the horse swaying to the clop of its hooves. She kept her hands folded in her lap, afraid if she said anything he would somehow turn their conversation to their marriage and all it entailed.

When he had entered the house earlier, he found her in the guest room. In no time at all, he had made it clear that was her room. No argument, no fight for her affection. "You can put your clothes in here." He indicated the hooks in the small closet. "And your other…items in the dresser. I hope it's cozy enough for your needs."

*What about your needs?* she longed to ask. Would he truly respect and keep his promise? And if they never grew to love each other, could they live a lifetime under these circumstances?

He startled her as he broke the silence. "You're very quiet this evening."

"Just thinking."

"About?"

She squirmed under his scrutiny. "About the fact that you have a lovely ranch. I had no idea when you offered to let me see your property. No idea at all. Do most of the ranchers hereabouts have such extensive properties?"

"Some."

She didn't know, but was pretty sure that small talk had never been her forte. And yet she'd try. "The sky is so clear. I can't wait for the stars to poke their heads out. I haven't seen anything as beautiful as your Western skies at night."

His gaze started at her head and ended at her feet. "It's lovely, all right."

Rebecca swallowed hard. "Are the winters long? I mean, very cold? What do you do to stay warm?" As soon as she asked, she wished she could take the question back. Why didn't she think before she opened her mouth?

His eyes narrowed. "Very cold. I air out the heavy quilts when winter arrives. And it usually arrives early hereabouts." He sighed. "Nights are most unbearable. It's not a good time to be alone."

She glanced from the corner of her eye. He sat straight, his jaw set, his eyes now fixed on the horizon. He was not being talkative as he had been the rest of the day. Ever since he came in from the barn. Was he angry?

"Is there also a lot of snow?"

"Plenty."

"Well, then. We'll never have to worry about a beautiful white Christmas."

"White Christmas, white Thanksgiving. If Mother Nature had her way, we'd have a white Fourth of July. The old-timers told me there was a hard frost one Fourth and lots of them lost all their corn and gardens." He turned to look her in the eye. "Our winters are harsh, Rebecca. Believe me, they are not for the faint of heart. There are nights when I swear if Cromwell didn't curl at my feet I'd freeze before morning."

"Cromwell?"

"A stray dog I took in when she was a pup. Don't worry, she's friendly. Goes about her own business most of the time."

"Cromwell, a she?" She shook her head. "I love dogs.

We had one when I was young. I don't remember what kind, but I remember having a dog."

"Well, a working ranch needs a good dog. Helps to frighten away wolves."

"Wolves?" She gasped. "Goodness, you would think you're trying to scare me into going back home."

"Whoa." He tugged hard on the reins, the muscles in his arms tightening in ripples against the cotton shirt he wore. She had never seen a man as thick with muscle that she could remember. He turned to face her. "This country is only for the strong. I am not exactly sure what you expected when you got aboard the train and headed West. This can be a very hard life, Rebecca. Many years, I am grateful to be here. Others, I'm not so sure. But if you have any doubts whatsoever, you need to speak up now, girl, or it *will* be too late. I have a good ranch, better than most, and yet my life is hard. I work morning to night, winters are cold, animals die, food is oftentimes scarce. We all spend every minute keeping our ranches afloat. You would be helping me to do that. But the life is not an easy one."

She cleared her throat against what she longed to say. If he thought for one minute she couldn't hold her own on the prairie, he was mistaken. Head raised, her chin jutted forward, she said, "I can assure you, Mr. Callahan, I am more than up to the challenge. Let us be honest with each other every step of the way. I have never backed down from hard work. Don't ask me how I know, I just do."

She sounded tough, even to herself, but if he turned her direction and yelled "boo," she would probably pass out from fright.

* * *

The woman had no idea what a challenge meant in this part of the country. A challenge meant fighting wolves to protect your stock, winters so ice-cold and snowy a man considered himself blessed merely to get to his barn and back alive without getting lost and freezing to death, food supplies scarce when the trains couldn't get through and no one but the person who shared your home to offer warmth and comfort—but he certainly wouldn't mention that little detail. With the kind of marriage he was signing on for, he figured on a lot more chilly nights with Cromwell snuggled against his feet.

He stole a glance at her. Like a princess in her royal carriage, Rebecca sat erect, hands folded in her lap in a grand ladylike style. Maybe he had taken on more than the bargain of the day.

She might be as cold as the winter. Cold didn't necessarily mean rough and tough. Was she up to the test of standing by his side, working a ranch? He didn't know more about her than a handful of letters could tell. Well, he'd read *Moby Dick,* and that didn't mean he understood the sea, did it? For all he knew, she might not be from a well-educated, wealthy family. She could be a criminal, pretending to be a woman named Rebecca Layne.

*Dear Lord, what have I gotten myself into? I pray You have control of this situation, because I seem to have lost my mind...over a woman.*

"I have no doubt you are up to any challenge." He grumbled more than spoke the words.

"Good. We have that behind us now. Well, Mr. Callahan, we've discussed the weather and your ranch. What shall we discuss now?"

His teeth ground against one another. She surely could rile a man. "Talk is overrated, *Miss* Layne." He eyed her sideways. "If that's your real name."

Her eyes sparked. "Very well. I guess I know when to curb my tongue. As for my name, I am at as much of a disadvantage as you are, sir."

*I doubt that.* Fingers tight on the leather, he slapped the reins and clucked to the horse. "Why don't we just enjoy the night sounds of the evening?"

As he stood knocking at the door of the justice of the peace, she swallowed over a lump the size of an apple. She would be marrying Jared Callahan, for sure and for true. No more Miss Layne. Or as he said, *if that's your real name.* Was it her name? Soon she would be Mrs. Jared Callahan. He rapped again at the door. Perhaps the man wouldn't marry them this late. Must be seven o'clock. She looked at the sky. Or later. Even though it was September, a chill already hung in the air. Probably just all his jabbering about the cold. The justice of the peace might be eating a wonderful dinner, one she could almost taste. Her mouth watered.

The front door opened with a loud scrape and Jared talked to a man, all the while motioning toward the buggy. The old fellow was all of five feet if he was an inch. Through the deepening dusk, all she could make out was a bushy head of white hair.

Mr. Callahan turned from the door, his steps dragging in the dirt. The man must have said no. So why the flitting butterflies of disappointment in her stomach? She knew why. She had actually begun to want this marriage with the man whose eyes called her name. Her fingers twisted in her lap, the letdown eating at her. She'd gone crazy. Did she actually want this marriage now?

Footsteps. She looked up suddenly.

"Let me help you down." He offered a hand.

"Is he going to marry us?" She choked on the words and drew her fingers to her mouth.

"He is."

"But you looked strange when you walked over here. As if…as if you were defeated somehow."

His mouth turned down at the sides in a sad expression. Like grief. "I had hoped this would be a joyous day, but now, well, we're both going to be making the best of it, aren't we?"

She pulled back. "And from that I am supposed to go with you? Mr. Callahan, how dare you? The best of it, indeed."

Now what did he say wrong? The woman had no sense. She said she wanted honesty? *Not likely.* Well, she'd made her feelings clear. She would be his servant, not his wife. So why did she have to raise his dander because he spelled the arrangement out plain as the wing on a fly? Women never had been his strong suit. Obviously. Otherwise he wouldn't have advertised for a bride. He'd have courted and made small talk with one of the town beauties, maybe even his widowed neighbor, Blanche, but no. He had a tough enough time just saying *hey* without tripping over himself.

Reaching for her arm once again, trying to make amends, he said, "Miss Layne. This is the last time I will ask whether or not you wish to go through with this marriage. If you are not fully committed to it, then we would be better off parting our ways right now. Let me buy you a ticket to…somewhere."

Was that hurt or anger on her face? "Mr. Callahan. Help me out of this buggy, if you please. I have never been one to go back on my word. Even when I find myself making a bargain with a rude, inconsiderate *farmer.* I'll thank you to help me down and escort me to the front door. Let's not make a scene in front of God…and…" her gaze shifted to the small house "…everyone." Her fingers sought his arm with a light touch, enough for him to feel the warmth through his sleeve but not enough to insinuate any familiarity.

He would have liked to cock a grin in her direction but thought better of making a fool of himself, so he sawed at his jaw, muscles so tight they felt like bands about to snap. Half the time he longed to grab her and hold her in his arms; other times, he wanted to lash out and put her in her place. Today, with a wedding about to be, he settled for his best manners. "Miss Layne," he said, covering her hand with his, "your obedient servant."

When they arrived at the door, the man with the wild hair smiled. A woman, a bit older than Methuselah, greeted them as well in a well-worn bathrobe. She continued to pluck strips of rags from her gray hair, wiry curls dangling in their place. "Dear me, a wedding. How lovely." Her face glowed as if this were the first wedding her husband had ever done. Maybe it was the first one ever done at night. "Mr. Brady, isn't this wonderful?"

"Wonderful, yes." The old fellow grinned and nodded, showing a lack of teeth along the back on both sides. "Simply wonderful."

Jared pulled his wallet from his pocket and placed a sawbuck in Brady's hand. "We've established that it's wonderful." He felt the scowl covering his face in spite of his efforts to smile along with all the *wonderful* comments. "Could we proceed with the ceremony?"

Rebecca's lip trembled. A sad expression replaced her anger. Not very gallant of him. He leaned closer to Rebecca, his hand twitching slightly as he guided her into the room. Surprised that her back didn't stiffen, he tried a smile, but her eyes now shot daggers into him. Whatever had bothered her, she'd recovered in a hurry. *Fine, let's keep it very impersonal.*

She murmured loud enough for all to hear, "Let's get this over with, shall we?"

He dropped his hand. "The sooner, the better. Mr. Brady, if you please."

Mrs. Brady, smelling of stale coffee and tapioca, blushed and stammered, "Oh my." Her lips pursed and Jared thought she might faint.

Instead, she pulled Rebecca to her side. Patting Rebecca's hand, she said, "My dear. Do you want this marriage?"

Rebecca stood as tall as a petite woman could. "Yes, ma'am." She addressed Mr. Brady. "It is getting late, don't you think? Perhaps we should get started." She gave the old woman a hug and a strained smile, then turned to take Jared's hand.

Her fingers looked deceiving—clean and well kept. He expected warmth, but her hand felt cold as a chunk of ice in a glass of lemonade.

Jared nodded. "Mr. Brady, if you please."

## Chapter 5

The ride back in the wagon included one bride, one groom and a cold chill that settled as thickly between them as an early, hard frost. Only difference was, a hard frost tended to make wild grapes sweeter; Jared could hardly be called sweet at the moment. Resigned was more like it. Stuck with her whether he wanted her or not.

Could she live with that arrangement?

Unsaid words clogged her throat. If she had any goodness in her, she would apologize for the scene at the justice of the peace's. After all, she had been the one to raise doubts in the folks' minds. When, oh, when would she learn to think before she spoke?

Her gaze skimmed over Jared. Dark, wavy hair. Coffee-brown eyes. Two huge dimples that lined his face when he smiled. He was as good-looking as anything. She longed to reach up and smooth the mussed hair on his forehead. Her hand shivered in her lap, but she quickly covered it with the other and settled against the wagon seat, all thoughts of the attractive groom pushed away from her. Besides, those dimples were well hidden behind a scowl. He looked like a bull about to charge. Well, he wasn't going to charge *her*. They'd both let their feelings be known. He had married her to give her a home and get himself a housekeeper. On that point, they were agreed, weren't they?

She sighed. If this was a real and true marriage, they would be celebrating, maybe a night in the hotel with a delicious hot dinner. Pot roast and potatoes, biscuits and jam. Mmm. She could taste it now. He might reach over afterward and hug her, kiss her. His thick, chiseled lips might speak her name in love. Her heart warmed, betraying her.

She slapped her hands together, brushing the issue away like spilled salt. It was done. They were married in name and nothing else. But what if…?

They *were* husband and wife.

She'd see to it he put her in the guest room. If not, she'd enforce the arrangement herself.

Why did she keep staring at him from the corner of her eye as if he were a thief ready to steal a bonbon from a store? Did she think he was going to pounce on her like a cat on a mouse? He had made it plain as the upturned nose on her conceited little face that he would leave her alone. He would work the ranch while she cared for the house. Nothing more. What a ridiculous arrangement. His own horse, an animal, wouldn't tolerate that; why should he? He blew out a blast of air.

Because he was a caring man who would never consider going back on his word.

A groan escaped his lips.

What sort of fool relationship had he agreed to? Only a complete idiot would make a bargain like that. Another groan squeezed from his chest.

She glanced at him. "Did you say something?"

He slapped the reins. "Nothing."

They passed the desolate area that Jared informed her was called Lone Rock. It stretched for half a mile. Her eyes grew round when she heard a noise crash over the edge. She leaned to the side and gripped the handrail. "What was that?"

"A chunk of rock broke loose, no doubt."

"How far down is that drop?"

"Too far for you to trek alone. I drove along this way because I wanted you to see this area. It's important you steer clear."

"The rocky cliff seems so out of place with the rest of the farmland around here."

"That it does. A very treacherous piece of ground. I used to take a mule down the ridge farther along, but don't think for one minute it would be safe for you to try." But never again, not since the fall. Nearly killed himself going after a lame foal. He needn't tell her about it. Would only worry her unnecessarily. He shook his head, his hair tumbling in his eyes. He swiped it away. "You just stay put on the ranch till you know your way around."

"I beg your pardon? Do you presume to tell me what to do?"

"I only meant… I meant…" *Infuriating woman! Calm down. She's afraid and doesn't know you. Give her time.* "Just until you know the lay of the land better. That's all I intended. You can't be running around willy-nilly getting yourself into trouble."

"You apparently intend quite a lot. And I'm not accustomed to getting myself in trouble."

*I don't intend anything. I would, if I could. But that isn't to be part of our arrangement, is it?* He stopped the buggy, exasperated as all get out. "Listen, are you going to argue about everything I say? I'm looking out for your own good. A man is supposed to take care of his wife. Protect her. I'm just trying to tell you these things so you don't go off half-cocked and hurt yourself." The mare pulled at the buggy and snorted. He tightened the reins. *Is every female so argumentative?*

She crossed her arms, eyes like flint. "I seem to have done all right so far in my life."

"Have you, now?" The absurdity of that statement brought him up short. Best to keep the chuckle to himself.

"You have the manners of a grizzly bear. If you would please stop talking to me and take me home." Her nose nearly reached the stars as she sat stiffly at his side. Lands, but his life had taken quite the turn tonight.

*Take her home?* This was her home. He had married her and intended to make her feel as comfortable as possible. As comfortable as she'd let him, anyway.

When they pulled up in front of the house, Jared offered his hand, but she brushed it aside. "Please," he said. "Allow me to help you down."

After a look that would have frightened his bull, Cantankerous, she held out her hand. Cold and stiff, her fingers touched his only long enough to descend from the buggy. If he'd been covered in lepers' spots, she couldn't have been more cautious. He had to find a way to make her feel as if this ranch was her home as well as his.

Carefully, so as not to scare her off, Jared draped an arm around her shoulder and tipped her chin with his thumb. "Look up, Rebecca. The stars. You said you loved the stars in our Western skies." None of them were as lovely as this woman, however. He longed to wrap her in both arms and kiss her until she saw stars, all right. He couldn't. "Well, now these are your skies, too."

She turned for the shortest moment and gazed at him. Was she having the same thoughts about the two of them? Perhaps if… No. He had promised. But her eyes sparkled with life and he had to catch his breath to steady his heartbeat and remember their deal. Was this the real Rebecca Layne? The one he had fallen in love with through her letters? *Letters…her letters.*

He slid his hand from her shoulder down to her fingers and led her along the path. "Let me help you to the porch swing, and while you enjoy our beautiful stars, I'll put on some coffee. Or, wait. You prefer tea, don't you?"

She smiled at him and then apparently thought better of it. "I'll have coffee with you. No need to change all the arrangements you're used to just for me. Coffee will do fine."

Here was the new Rebecca again. He grumbled over the sound of his boots. She liked tea and by all the goodness in the world, she was going to get tea!

Jared stepped inside and for the first time since he had built the house, everything looked different to him. Looked like a house a man had been baching it in. Out of place in a strange way, as if something were missing. *Rebecca.*

He put the coffee on to warm and another smaller kettle of hot water for tea. Then he stole to the guest room. With great care he took Rebecca's letters from the dresser. Choosing the first one he had received from her, he sniffed the perfume and longed for the loving woman at the other end. After daydreaming, he scribbled on the back, "I thought you might like to read this. Perhaps it will help you remember. Your obedient servant, Jared." And that's all he was now, an obedient servant. He didn't love this woman as he had loved the Rebecca of the letters, but perhaps in time.

She closed her eyes. She could feel the beauty of the country all about her. The swing, which he'd told her he'd built as a wedding gift, swayed gently, the breeze it created tickling her hair. Crickets chirped under the porch and a lone howl sounded in the direction of the desolate drop he'd shown her. A sharp barking startled her and she drew her legs under her instead of pushing the swing. What a strange land. Beautiful and frightening all at the same time. The night air, according to Jared, balmy for this time of year, filled her lungs with freshness. Everything about this country, with one exception, spoke to her heart. And if truth be told, he was beginning to work his way into her heart, as well. But she could never let him know that. Her husband already had her at a terrible disadvantage. He knew who he was. What his life meant.

And yet, like it or not, this was her life now, too. She would do her best to make the home comfortable for

him, even though their lives might never truly be as
husband and wife. In time, could they find a way to…

The door closed with a light thump, startling her.

"I'll be off to the barn, then. Water's on the stove.
For your *tea*. Should be hot by now. Help yourself."

Oh, why was she dreaming? He would continue to
work the ranch and she would be his loyal housekeeper
because he'd saved her from being homeless. Nothing
more than that. But at least she had this place to call
home. After what she'd faced in town recently, a safe
home seemed almost like heaven. The thought of Mr.
Fletcher, the way he looked at her, caused chills to rip-
ple over her arms and down her back. Goose bumps
and shivers. Yes, marrying Jared had been the wise
thing to do.

Once she removed her bonnet and smoothed her hair,
her feet, like slabs of iron, drew her to the kitchen in
search of the tea. A small crystal bowl filled with white
sugar sat next to a matching creamer he had left filled
to the top.

She poured the hot liquid into a cup and made her
tea. Drawing in a deep breath, she sniffed the steam,
and the smell offered its own form of comfort. When
she began adding sugar and cream, it made her think of
home. She must have loved tea. The thought of drinking
that thick brown coffee everyone seemed to want out
here sent a shiver rippling through her. A lady always
drank tea. The taste, sweet and creamy, warmed her
from her cold hands to her feet. He'd put the water on
for her. A kindness she hadn't expected. If truth be told,
he'd been kinder than she ever could have imagined.

Taking her cup with her, she padded to the guest room.
A lit kerosene lamp already spread a soft glow of

light throughout the room. He had thought of everything. She had not given him one single consideration. How cold she had grown since the train accident. Or maybe she had always been an uncaring woman. How could she know for sure? Perhaps, in time, the real Rebecca Layne would emerge and she'd know where she belonged and with whom.

*Oh, God. Help me, please. I need to be able to at least be a helpmate to Jared.*

God? Was she a praying woman? Well, of course she was. Wasn't everyone?

She shook her head and turned.

A rumpled letter lay on the thick pillow at the head of the bed. She set down the cup of tea and picked up the page. Well worn. From much reading?

*April 10, 1882*
*Dear Mr. Callahan,*
*I have read your ad in the paper for a bride, and while I must say I am intrigued by your interest, I am much surprised that I sit here so easily writing to you.*

*Let me tell you about myself. My name is Rebecca Layne. I am a well-educated woman of twenty years who has tired of life in the city. I do have a family, but their desire is for me to stay in the East and marry well. Whatever that means when discussing matters of the heart, I'm sure I do not know.*

*I have longed for the West since first reading tales of it in school. I am a restless sort and am anxious to find myself far from here.*

*And a ranch. My, but that does sound so very*

*exciting. I would like so much if you could write
to me and tell me about yourself other than that
you are a "hardworking rancher." Might I know
more about you?*
*Anxiously awaiting your kind response,*
*Rebecca Layne*

She smelled the paper; a faint scent of lilacs once
again filled her nose. Had she written this letter? She
did love lilacs.

She glanced about for something with which to write.
A small pen and ink sat atop the dresser. She turned the
letter over and tried with her injured hand to write her
name. The letters appeared nothing like the signature
on the stationery. Perhaps it would have to wait until
her hand had healed completely.

A small rap at the door drew her attention. "Did you
have your tea?"

Was he coming in? Her heart hammered.

"Yes, thank you." She quickly put away the ink and
the letter. No reason for him to know she'd been foolish enough to try and sign her name.

"Then I'll close up for the night. I start early, around
five in the morning. It's been a long day. You might
want to sleep in tomorrow and start at lunchtime."

"But I thought—"

"Give your body a chance to heal, Rebecca. There
will be plenty of time to help with chores."

*Help with chores? Of course. That's why he mar-
ried me.*

## Chapter 6

A wide yawn split his face. He shut his mouth and looked around. No one to notice but Charger.

Tired from a night of no sleep thinking of Rebecca a mere ten or so feet from him, Jared grabbed the curry-comb. Rubbing much too briskly, he irritated Charger enough that the horse turned and nipped at his hand. Wasn't the horse's fault.

"Sorry, boy. Do *you* understand females? Of course not. I've seen how you act when I turn you out with pretty little Tinker or the flirt, Isabelle. You behave the fool just like I'm acting. I wish I understood how females think. No, no. That would be a bad idea. No man wants to know what a female thinks. Not really, if he's honest with himself."

He rubbed the stallion's sides, with a softer touch this time. "There isn't one of us who'd want to admit he understood them, boy. Don't you feel bad, now. You get a whiff of that pretty little filly and turn into a fool. It's all right. I catch the scent of lemon verbena and I'm no better." Charger flicked his head back and Jared whipped his hand out of the way. "Don't get upset with me. I hate to admit it, but the same thing happens to me. To any man who's attracted to a female. We all turn into blithering idiots. Trying to figure out what they want. What they like, don't like. Whether they look to us for protection or get the idea we're trying to control them."

Jared stopped brushing. He nipped the edge of his lip and froze in thought. What do they want? Think? Hope?

He growled from deep in his chest like a frightened coyote. An ad in a paper. A handful of letters. And now a wife. He'd never been more confused.

Charger swiveled his head back again, this time with a look that said he somehow shared Jared's pain. "There you go, boy. Have some oats and then we'll head to town, one last time for a while. With crops about ready and hay all set to bring in, I'll be busier than an ant at a summer picnic. When we ride back, it'll be just you and me, like always." He scratched Charger's mane and rubbed him gently until his coat shone. Then Jared whispered in his ear, "Only now we got a couple of women to care for. Think we can manage, old friend?"

He finished mucking the stalls and laying straw. Then he filled the troughs with fresh hay, checked Tinker's leg and slopped the hogs. The cows had been milked first thing. When he'd put the milk down in the cellar, Rebecca had been asleep. At least, with her door closed he guessed she was still sleeping even though it had been well past seven in the morning. He'd told her to sleep in, not waste an entire day.

Fall breezes flicked dust against the side of the barn. He'd have to put bales of straw around the perimeter soon. Hard to tell when a Minnesota snowstorm might wallop them unexpectedly. And despite the balmy days, the nights were already growing steadily cooler. Jared was grateful the town was less than three miles away. Less chance of being surprised by an early storm. Today, if she ever rolled out of bed, he'd ask Rebecca if there were any goods she wanted for the kitchen. Then he'd head to town and back, giving her the chance to become accustomed to her new home.

"Okay, fella." He slapped Charger on the rump. "It's you and me for the day. I'll harness the buggy and you can follow along behind at your own pace. No rush. I'll pick up a few odds and ends, some nails and maybe grab an apple for you along the way. How's that sound?"

Charger nickered. Maybe he understood after all.

She heard the thump of his boots on the porch. Glad she had thought to start his lunch, even though eleven was a bit early, she turned at the sound of his voice. She'd get it on the table right away if he wanted.

"Rebecca?"

"In here." She tried for a genuine smile not accompanied by a yawn, but she was sure her face seemed more of a lopsided smirk.

"Smells wonderful. Soup?"

"I foraged through your supplies. I hope it was all right that I used your leftover slab of cold beef from the cellar. This should be ready around noon. Is that time all right or are you hungry now?"

"Noon or a little after, even. I'm in no rush."

"Is it all right that I used—"

He held up a hand to stop her. "None of this is mine. Everything on this ranch is yours as well, Rebecca." He ruffled his fingers through his hair. "One of the reasons I wanted to speak with you."

*Oh no. Here it comes. He realizes his mistake and I'm to be turned out. Where will I go?*

"You look pale. What's wrong?" He held out a chair. "Here, sit down."

She put down the wooden spoon and her hand went immediately to her chest. She sat and nodded. "Why did you want to talk to me?" As if she couldn't discern the face he made. It said clear as day *you're going home, little lady.*

"To ask if there's anything I can get you in town. You've had a chance to go through the pantry. Can I pick up any supplies? Any doodads you might need for...I don't know what."

*Doodads?* A smile tugged at her lips. "I did notice your coffee is low. If you'd be kind enough to buy some coffee...perhaps a pound of raisins, as well. I'd like to be able to bake apple pie this autumn, and I always mix in a few raisins." She stopped. Did she have the right to ask for things he didn't ordinarily use? She had no money to give him. Maybe while in town he would buy her, not raisins, but a ticket to nowhere. She should shut up and simply say there was nothing she needed. She had been given a roof over her head and food in her stomach. What more did she expect from this sham of a marriage?

His brow drew close, deepening the crevice between his eyes. Maybe she'd made him angry. She seemed good at that. She shouldn't have used the piece of beef.

He took her hand in his. "Come here, Rebecca."

She rose as he led her to the small crock in the corner. Now she'd done it. "What did I do wrong?"

"Nothing. Here." He reached in and pulled out a handful of silver dollars. "Rebecca, you may go to town whenever you choose. You may purchase whatever you choose. This is your home now and everything that's in it is yours."

Jared placed the money in her hand, and then turned to leave. She thought she heard the faintest grumble. "Including me."

Had she heard him? He toed the ground in anger. Nothing like lovesickness to turn him into a pathetic excuse for a man. And what had possessed him to say *doodads?* He had not used that word once in his life. Doodads? He must have sounded like a rambling fool. Well, he'd get her raisins, all right. A whole bagful. And anything else that looked appealing. He intended to make every effort to be a kind and loving husband. *But, God, what does that mean? I've never been a husband before. How can I be what I don't understand? Don't couples generally learn together what it means to be husband and wife? Hand in hand, together as one? We're more like a circus act that doesn't know how to perform without a ringmaster. Help me, here.*

With the rented buggy ready and Charger tied to the back, Jared set off for town, his emotions as bumpy and rumbly as the road. Still questioning each word he had said to her since they'd returned to the ranch from town, he heaved a grunt worthy of Cantankerous. He didn't know one thing about women. Thought he did, but he was wrong. The letters had opened a door to a new life and shut it just as surely. He slapped the reins.

He had to stop second-guessing himself. This situation was what it was. They were married, and this was his new life: tied to a woman who tugged at his heart but might never want to be part of it.

He turned his attention to the weather. No rain. Good. Keep it dry till he got all the hay stacked. Another sunny day. One he should spend working in the field. Maybe that kid who helped Duncan Ketch would be willing to earn a silver dollar for a week's hard labor. Another man to assist him in bringing in the hay would be such a blessing. He couldn't ask a woman to throw hay bales. Although she would no doubt try her best just to prove him wrong if he mentioned it. Hmm, that would make a wonderful experiment—learning exactly how obstinate a woman could be.

He grinned ear to ear and started whistling a tune.

Rebecca drew in a long breath. The fresh bread smelled delicious; the clock had struck twelve as she pulled it from the oven some time ago. A trip to the cellar had produced a cloth-covered plate with a large ball of butter in the middle. *Lands, does he make his own butter? A man shouldn't have to do that.* She slid a finger over the top and plopped it in her mouth. Sweet and fresh. How wonderful it would taste on a slice of the warm bread.

The soup, thick and aromatic, bubbled and spit on the stove. And what a stove it was. Four burners, a huge oven and an overhead warming space. She could bake the bread and keep it hot while waiting for lunch to begin. She hadn't ever seen a stove like it. Had she?

She hoped he wouldn't be too late or the bread would be cold. Searching the drawers in the hutch, she found a cloth and wrapped the loaf. There. Now all would be ready when he arrived home. Home to his wife, Rebecca Callahan. But he'd look at her like a chore girl. Instead of seeing a reflection of love in his heavenly eyes, she would see her boss, the man who had hired her.

Collapsing against the counter, she drummed the edge with her fingertips. Being called Rebecca when she didn't know whether or not she *was* a Rebecca irritated the bloomers off her. She had to find a way around that other woman's name. And it didn't really matter if she was the other woman.

Becca. That would do it. She would ask to be called Becca.

At the prospect of finally having her own name, a song sprang to her lips.

"Do I hear singing?"

She hadn't heard him come in. Startled, Becca stopped. "You're here."

"I am. And I brought a few bags of supplies. As much as Charger would allow me to haul back. But that's for later. Right now I smell fresh bread, and I'm a starving man, Rebecca."

"Becca."

He searched her face. "What?"

"I'd like to be called Becca. That way I have my own name, not one I don't recognize."

"Why, it's all one and the same, isn't it?"

She pulled bread from the warming bin and shot him a frown as she unwrapped it. "Not to me, it isn't. This way, I'll have something that's my very own, at least until I know for sure who I am."

His eyes darkened in a way that drew her in. "I know who you are. You're Mrs. Jared Callahan."

Ignoring the intimate comment, she plated the bread, put it next to the butter on the table and ladled soup into the bowls she'd found in the cupboard. "These look too pretty for every day. Don't you have other dishes?"

Holding her chair out, Jared shook his head. "These were my mother's. I saw no reason to buy any others."

"Your mother's. Well, I'll be sure and take great care with them."

Once again, he took her hand in his. "You need to stop worrying so much, Reb—Becca. I realize this is a strange way to begin a marriage, but it is a marriage, and all that I have belongs to you, as well. Be yourself here. There will be long hours of hard work. You need to be able to know this is your home. You should find comfort in these walls. Including whether or not a cup or saucer slips and breaks. No matter."

He cut a slice of bread from the loaf and dipped a piece in his soup. Licking his lips, he said, "Now, this is what food is supposed to taste like. Thank you."

No contrary comments came to her mind. She was pleased. In fact, she found herself appreciating his compliment so much, a smile quivered across her face.

Was that a smile? Jared glanced again from the corner of his eyes. By Jiminy, it was a smile.

He smacked the remaining drops of the soup. The last time he'd had such a delicious meal, other than at Millie's, was before he left Olivia's. And in her day, his mother had cooked the best fried chicken—could stretch a meal farther than a mile when strangers showed up at the door.

A sigh of satisfaction escaped him. "I appreciate the lunch. Now, what say we take a peek at the packages

I brought from town?" His eyebrows lifted playfully. "There might be some surprises."

Becca didn't try to hide her amusement as he loaded her arms with raisins, coffee, white sugar, vanilla, tea and numerous containers of spices. Things he hadn't used but knew she would, as they made food taste that much better.

After she had put the all the packages away, he dug a box from his inside pocket. How would she react? "Come sit down. I have a surprise."

She fingered a curl that had loosened at the side of her head. "What's that?"

"A gift." Here. He held the small box at arm's length. "I thought you should have one."

Her gaze, a question mark, leveled onto the box. She opened the velvety top and gasped. But her eyes filled with tears and she dropped it. Without a word, she dashed from the room.

*Now* what had he done? He figured, since they were legally married and all, she should have the wedding ring he'd ordered. No sense letting tongues wag in town.

Jared walked into the front room and slumped in his chair. This past week had been tiring. And the more he tried to figure her out, the more he ached, physically and mentally. Each day was filled with indecision and feelings running from one side to the other. Charger and Cantankerous had easier lives. They only had to deal with females during mating season. And then the females understood their duties as well as the males.

*Mating season?* His face heated and he swallowed hard. Popping the ring into his pocket for the second time that day, he blew out a loud breath. He needed to go to the barn, where he could think on other things. Things that a man understood.

Becca allowed the tears to flow. She didn't care if he heard her, was upset with her or wanted her to leave. How could he understand? He knew who he was. Jared Callahan. Jared Ezekiel Callahan. He had a mother and a father who had passed away when he was young. His sister, Olivia, had raised him and seen him through school back East. He'd traveled West because he loved open spaces and animals. He'd told her so. His ranch did well for the most part because of his hard work, so she wouldn't want for anything, at least, not the necessities.

What did she have to offer? No name, no past, nothing to speak of but her ability to cook and keep house. How she remembered that, she wasn't sure. Was there a brother or sister out there somewhere? A husband? A child, even? It was possible she had married Jared and had no right. Now to wear a ring as proof. How *could* he understand? If he lived in her shoes for just a few minutes, he might understand how afraid she was.

She shuddered and the tears started afresh. She might be an adulteress! Lands, what would Grandma Ellis have to say about that?

*Grandma Ellis?*

Did Rebecca Layne have a Grandma Ellis? Or did she, Becca Callahan, have a sweet old lady she called Grandma Ellis?

She squeezed her eyes tight, but no picture of the grandmotherly woman came to mind. Yet she *had* remembered the name. It must mean something.

Later that evening after a painfully long silence in front of the huge stone fireplace, Becca retired.

Jared didn't say a word other than, "Good night."

As she closed the door, she peeked at him through the crack. Those deep brown, almost charcoal eyes shone in the firelight. His hair, which she should cut soon, hung in a thick mass over his ears and on his neck. As if he sensed her peeping at him, his hand drew up and riffled through the shaggy mane.

Becca closed the door. Memories of an old lady with gray hair swirled through her thoughts while she donned her flannel nightgown. She had to connect to her past. How? How would she find out who Becca Callahan really was? And as each day passed, did she care as much? Perhaps she was beginning to like her life with Jared more than a little bit.

The lamp in her room once again had been lit for her, offering its special cozy light. And once again…Becca found another letter on her pillow as she readied for bed.

# Chapter 7

April 29, 1882

Dear Mr. Callahan,

I was very pleased to receive your kind letter so soon. And I must tell you that I grow more anxious each day to be able to finish all of my business here and travel on the next train to the West. Since my twenty-first birthday is July 1, my parents can no longer force me to remain in Boston and marry someone I don't choose to love.

Your ranch sounds so appealing. I am anxious to meet both Tinker and Charger. Will Tinker allow me to ride her, do you think? We will have such fun dashing across the prairie side by side. I can picture us now.

Oh, please excuse me if I sound too forward. It

*is just that your letters are filled with much con-
tentment and I feel as if I've known you a long time.*

*You asked me what I look like. Does that mat-
ter? I am laughing here, pretending to think you
don't care. Well, Mr. Callahan, I cannot say myself, but I am told I'm rather attractive. I have
blond hair and blue eyes, though to me, that is
so ordinary I might need to think about this before I say any more. I'm rather trim and petite.
Do you believe that? I might be as ample as my
aunt Grace and you would never know it until I
arrived. I am teasing you again, Jared. I hope
you don't mind. I love to laugh.*

*You have not told me if you are as handsome
as your letters sound.*

*Will Charger and Tinker be proud to have us
riding them for all the world to see?*

*My sister knocks at the door. I'll have to write
more later.*
*Anxiously awaiting your loving response,*
*Rebecca Layne*

From a kind to a loving response. A rather forward
girl, but it was obvious she cared a great deal about
him already. Why was it that not one word in the letters sounded familiar? Another visit to Dr. Parker might
be in order. He did tell her it might be weeks or even
months before she remembered. *If* she remembered at
all.

Becca walked to the small mirror on the wall above
her dresser. She stared at the image. Blond hair, blue
eyes. Attractive? Perhaps she could be called attractive.

But would she ever write that to a stranger? Were these, in fact, her words on the paper?

She lifted the brush from the dresser top and pulled it through her hair. Jared had purchased the dressing-table set for her before they'd left town. He had bought every single item she needed, and it pained her to be so indebted to the man. And the ring. Such an elaborate gesture.

Her curls resisted her efforts. So she set the brush down and allowed her finger to trace her lips while the girl in the mirror, with an inquisitive glance, asked her what she wanted. Tilting her head to the side, she whispered, "Are you Rebecca Layne?" Her head shook. "Rebecca Callahan. Are you? Or are you a stranger who just happened along?" *Oh, poor Jared. He has a past, while I have nothing to bring to this marriage.*

Did it really matter? Maybe he only wanted someone to share chores with. How disconcerting not to know precisely what he expected. And yet they didn't spend a lot of time talking, making the kinds of decisions that would guide their lives.

She lifted the brush and continued stroking her hair in an ever-increasing rhythm. Fifty-seven, fifty-eight. She might be the woman in the letters. Becca stopped counting. Her eyes *were* blue. Very blue, in fact. Her father had called them bluebell blue.

*Her father!* "My little Blue Belle." He'd laughed and tossed her in the air.

*Belle.* He'd called her Belle. And it certainly seemed she was close to him. A happy family. Could Belle be a nickname for Rebecca?

Her heart thrummed in her chest. The pieces were beginning to come to life. Perhaps, if she kept reading the letters, she'd discover who she really was…or wasn't. She tensed. When she glanced down, she saw blood. Her palm had grasped the bristles so tightly they had cut into the healing wound. Like her heart, a huge, empty, gaping wound.

Jared kicked his boots across the floor. If only she could remember. They might make a life for themselves and be happy. Maybe. If only… Oh, why lament the if-only? *God, where do I go from here? You know who she is. Why can't You tell me? Her husband.*

As he mentally checked off the chores for tomorrow, his hand came to rest on his chin. This wasn't exactly the dream he'd imagined when first he'd written to Rebecca asking her to come out. It had turned into more of a nightmare.

When he plopped on the edge of the bed, his gaze shifted to the other side. He shouldn't be alone on this overly plump feather tick. Cromwell lifted her head. Her whiskers drew down on the sides, but still, he swore she laughed at him. One more woman with the upper hand.

"Get down!"

Cromwell jumped down, turned around twice on the braided rug and slumped to the floor, but her eyes tipped at the edges as if her feelings were hurt. She grunted in a whoosh of air and put her head on her paws.

Jared leaped to his feet and began pacing. This was no way to live out a marriage. Promises or not.

As he turned back to the bed, he noticed Cromwell had crept back to the warm spot where she'd slept before. He didn't even have control of the mutt.

Becca listened to the heavy footfalls clomping from one end of the house to the other. Did he pace his room every night? Having to arise so early, he should stop all this nonsense, curl under the covers and try to stay warm.

There was still plenty of fresh bread for breakfast. A bowl of hen's eggs sat on the counter away from the stove. In the morning, she would raw-fry some potatoes to go with the warm bread and eggs. Later, if she had the chance, she would pick some apples and think about applesauce or fresh pie.

As she finished deciding what she would fix for breakfast, the pacing stopped. She placed her hand against the wall where she realized the head of his bed rested. Could he sense her presence on the other side?

Within minutes, she heard a soft rumbling through the wall. Not an intruding snore, but enough for her to know he was there. Oddly enough, the sound comforted her.

*You asked me what I look like. Does that matter?*

A flush skittered across her face and she jerked her hand back. No sense dwelling on things that shouldn't be.

Weeks later, once they'd settled into a comfortable routine, Jared rode past the porch with tools dangling at Charger's side. He shouted over his shoulder, "I'll be gone most of the day. Don't look for me before supper."

Becca realized she had the entire day to herself; she figured she'd make the best of it. Sitting on the porch swing, the sun barely peeking over the rail, she let her gaze roam from one side of the ranch as far as she could see to the other. Grass and wildflowers still grew thick and green in front of the house. Without considering the cold, crisp morning, she took off her boots and stockings and walked through the carpet of grass. As the sun poured over the yard, golden and bright, she dropped down and lay in the sweet clover. This she understood. Men? Not so much. At least, she didn't think so. Who knew what she might have left behind? Her eyes closed almost of their own accord with the sun strong now.

How long had she lain there, soaking up the last of the warmth? Too long. Chores waited. Applesauce didn't make itself while she lolled in the grass.

A shadow covered her and a shiver ran the length of her body. Jared must have decided to come back early. He'd find her wasting time. How could she explain that?

"Well, if it isn't *Mrs.* Callahan."

Becca opened her eyes and jumped to her feet. She smoothed her skirt, all the while her heart hammering as she recognized Mr. Fletcher. "That's right. What's your business here?"

Hat removed, he lowered into a mock bow. "I came to see you, dear lady."

"I doubt my husband will be happy to see you on his property." Her fingers rubbed the edge of her skirt, a nervous habit she'd been unable to break.

Fletcher laughed. "I saw him ride away not an hour ago as I was leaving the Cains'. I had an…appointment with Blanche."

"But Jared said—"

"Her husband passed on nine months ago. That's right. I was simply helping out. With the chores, you know. Women can't do all the things a man can." He smirked.

Becca immediately gazed at her hands, afraid to look him in the eye and see that expression of his that made her feel…uncovered. "My, but you are the helpful one, aren't you?"

She glanced toward the barn, hoping, but she knew Jared wasn't working there today. "You have no right to be here, Mr. Fletcher. My husband will be angry if you don't go now."

"I rather doubt that, m'lady. You remember, I saw him ride off this morning."

A deep voice punctuated the air. "Too bad you didn't see me return." Jared's hand clamped down on Fletcher's wrist. He wrenched the unwelcome guest's arm behind him and pushed him toward his horse.

"I know your kind, Fletcher. Don't ride this way again. It's my property." He looked in Becca's direction. "Along with everything on it."

Her hair bristled at her neck. She was no one's property. But she wouldn't broach that topic, not here, not now. After all, he *had* just saved her life, and maybe her virtue.

As Fletcher rode off, Jared turned. "I left my lunch in the barn. You looked like you could use a bit of help."

She lifted her nose in the air. "I'm sure I could have taken care of myself."

"Yes, ma'am. That is just what it looked like. You don't know men like Fletcher, Becca. He runs the saloon in town. Now, I'll grab my lunch and leave you to your own devices."

"He runs the what?" But he'd said…

Not a thank-you, not the hint of a smile. No good deed went unpunished. Wasn't that what Olivia used to tell him? But God didn't work that way. Didn't play those games. And yet this entire arrangement seemed like a colossal game of some sort. He had to ask himself—did he want to play?

All the letters, the hopes, the dreams. They had planned their lives right down to the number of children they might have. Four. An Olivia after his sister. A William, a Charles and an Emma. And more horses. Rebecca said she loved horses, but now…that bump on her head had obviously brought about a great deal of change in her. Oh, well, he had work to attend to. Fences to fix. He did not have time to contemplate the mind of this woman. His wife.

Dwelling on the two words—his wife—he barely heard the hissing. Charger balked, reared his head in the air and stomped his foot. A snake! Jared jerked hard on the reins and shouted at Charger. But, eyes wild, his whites begging for help, the horse leaped straight up, dumping Jared off the saddle and onto the ground. He heard a crunch and pop when Charger landed on his ankle. Then a searing pain shot up the calf of his leg. Jared groaned and rolled to his side to catch his breath. Bright sun began to dim until all he saw was black.

Becca fumed all afternoon about being called Jared's property. She'd have plenty to discuss with him when he returned to the house. Apparently she didn't even have the position of housekeeper, because if she did, she wouldn't be thought of as property. A housekeeper could up and quit on his sorry self. She couldn't quit, couldn't find other work, couldn't afford to lose the only home she had. Wait till supper. She'd serve him, all right. She'd serve him a healthy recipe of opinions. And he'd eat them or starve.

Clouds rolled in as the day wore on, but no rain.

Eventually the fluffy whiteness passed over the ranch and her anger ebbed. She hadn't expected him for lunch, but the late afternoon brought no sign of him, either. Where was he?

She waited an hour later than usual before finally eating her supper. The beans had baked hot and thick with drizzles of molasses and honey over the top. Chunks of salt pork browned in the sweet goodness until they lured her to the table. But even if Jared had lost track of time, he would surely be hungry by now. It hadn't taken her long to learn his stomach functioned as an accurate timepiece. Six for breakfast, noon for dinner and six for supper. Just like that. Not a minute one way or the other unless something came up.

A few minutes after she ate the last bite of corn bread, she washed the dainty flowered cup she'd used for tea and set it to dry next to the stove. Much longer and she would need to move the beans off the stove, where she'd kept them warming for Jared. Glancing around the cheerful kitchen, she placed a hand against her stomach. Flips and twangs ate at her gut, telling her something was very wrong. Her stomach didn't do these leaps and lurches for no reason. And it had nothing to do with her anger earlier.

The light outside had begun to dim. Soon it would be time to tend to the night's chores. She'd been watching Jared milk the cow and saddle the horses, but she didn't feel confident that she could do those things yet. The chores would have to wait for Jared.

Dusk settled more quickly, and Becca couldn't wait another minute for Jared to come home. He had to be in trouble. She moved the beans aside, set the coffee on the front where it would stay warm but not boil dry then pulled her fichu around her shoulders. Insides tumbling harder now, she sprinted toward the barn to saddle and ride Tinker whether Tinker's leg would allow it or not. But Charger rounded the side of the building before she could hoist the wood from the latch. Empty saddle. No Jared. And Charger stomped and snorted.

Without a thought to her own safety, Becca dived for the mighty beast. She calmed him for only a few seconds and then hauled herself up. Straddling the animal like a man, she kicked her heels. "Where is he, boy? Where's Jared?" Charger knew where to lead. He pounded the ground without once looking back to the warmth and food that shelter meant. He seemed to know Becca was needed.

About ten minutes later, they rounded a grove of trees on the farthest side of the property and Becca saw a silhouetted figure on the ground. She leaped from Charger and dropped to her knees. "Jared!"

Eyes bloodshot and swollen, he gazed at her, but trying to lift his arm was too much of an effort and he drifted away again.

"Are you all right?" She leaned closer to see if his breathing was steady. *Oh, please let him be all right.* "What hurts?"

"Becca?" The word whooshed in her ear. "Get help."

She pulled his head onto her lap. "I'm afraid to move you, Jared."

His laugh was manna to her. Alive. That's all that mattered.

"You'll have to…go."

"What happened?"

He licked his lips. "Snake." Jared drew in a deep breath and coughed. "Charger threw me."

"Where are you injured?" She looked down and spied the split along the side of his pants. Black and blue marks ran from his calf to his ankle, where a jagged rock and his horse had done their damage. She picked up the rock and threw it. Charger jumped.

"Whoa…fella." Jared glanced in Becca's direction, eyes wide with pain. "Better keep him calm. When I fell…knocked the air out." He flinched. "My ribs, my leg. Need help, Becca."

"You've lost a lot of blood. I think we'd better get you back to the house."

"No." He struggled to sit up, but couldn't. "You can't move me…not by yourself. Probably a lot worse than it looks." He ground his cheek with his teeth. "Get Blanche." His breathing became more shallow now. She leaned closer. "She's near. Please, Becca. Hurry."

She tore off her fichu, put it under his head and dashed for Charger again. "I'll be right back."

"Becca!"

The Cain Ranch. Wasn't that less than a mile up the road? "Come on, boy." She dug her heels into the animal's sides and prayed he had enough energy left to get her to Blanche Cain's ranch.

# Chapter 8

Mrs. Cain sat on the front porch in an old wooden swing, her red hair in a thick braid over her shoulder, bobbing in time with the squeaky swing. This was the widow Cain? Becca had expected an older woman, not a young woman Jared's age. In the lantern light Becca could see that she was beautiful. Mrs. Cain placed a hand on her eyes, searching the darkness. "Well, hello, Charger. Who's your friend?"

No time to dwell on green eyes, Becca jumped to the ground and threw the reins over the porch rail. "Do you have a wagon? Mrs. Cain, we need help!"

The woman rose from the swing, pulling her sweater closer. "Settle down. Let me look at you, girl." She drew her gaze from Becca's toes to her hair. "I heard about you. Jared Callahan's new hired girl. Is that right?"

Now wasn't the time to set her straight. She needed

to make her understand that Jared's life was in danger. "Jared's hurt bad. I need a wagon to move him." A shiver rippled across her shoulders and she gripped her arms over her chest.

Blanche Cain jumped off the edge of the porch. "Well, why didn't you say so? Let's get a move on."

She took over immediately. She ran toward the barn, and in a matter of minutes pulled a buckboard into view alongside Becca. "Here. Take this jacket or you'll freeze to death." She threw an old work jacket at Becca, which she gratefully put on before mounting Charger again. "You lead me. Go slow enough, now, so I can follow you in the dark."

Becca's lip trembled. "All right."

Wagon wheels stirred the dusty ground, but Becca heard his voice, weaker than a mewling calf. "Over... here."

"Mrs. Cain. He's under that tree. He said Charger fell on him. Anyway, I think he's broken his leg—or worse."

"There's not a whole lot worse."

"Well, I meant he's lost a lot of blood."

Mrs. Cain jumped down from the wagon and drew to his side as if—as if she knew him very well. "My, Jared Callahan." She laid her fingers on his forehead. "How on earth did you get yourself into a fix like this?"

He smiled and lifted a hand to hers. "Blanche. Your hired man, Dort, with you? I think...I'm gonna need more help...than you can be."

"Depends on what you need, darlin'." She laughed at her comment.

"Dort?"

"I let him go. But don't you mind about that right now." Was Jared smiling again, happy she'd gotten rid of the help? "Between your new girl here and me, we'll get you onto the wagon and into bed. First thing in the morning, she can ride into town, fetch Doc Parker." She kneaded his leg a moment longer than Becca thought appropriate and shook her head. "I don't believe you've broken it, just torn a lot of flesh. But you're bleeding something fierce. Can you lean on me if I hoist you to your feet?"

"Not sure."

"Come here, missy," Mrs. Cain ordered. "Let's try to take all his weight on us. Then we'll haul him into the wagon. Get him to my place. It's closest."

Becca started to complain, but stopped. Mrs. Cain spoke the truth. Her place bordered Jared's near where he'd fallen and he wouldn't have to be jarred as much. "All right. Show me what to do."

Lifting him was more difficult than Becca thought it would be. Because he kept passing out, he was deadweight for the two of them. But Becca surprised herself before they were done. Almost as if she'd done this before. She braced her legs and heaved as Mrs. Cain hauled him over the side.

Once he was in the wagon, the woman pulled a blanket over Jared and rolled another for under his head. "There you go. Think you can make it all right?"

With a smile, he murmured, "Don't see...as I have much choice. Thanks, Blanche. I've always...been able to count on you."

Becca bit down on her lip to keep from asking the obvious. He might have counted on Blanche far too much before Becca arrived. No, he wouldn't have advertised for a bride if the neighbor woman appealed to him.

"That's what neighbors are for." She glanced Becca's way. "Let's get moving. We haven't got all night."

Cheeks blazing hot, Becca tucked her fichu under the edge of the saddle, tied Charger to the back of the wagon and climbed in next to Jared. Mrs. Cain drove the rig slowly as Becca supported Jared as best she could.

Once they arrived at the ranch, he turned his head to Becca. "After I'm settled, can you go back to the ranch and take care of the night chores? I'm sorry, Becca… but I can't…let the animals suffer."

She looked from Jared to Mrs. Cain and back again. He would stay here alone with this woman. This redhead with eyes the color of emeralds. A widow. "All right. I'll come back as soon as—"

"No need," Mrs. Cain said. "Just go get Doc Parker soon as you're done."

Jared shouted, "No! Blanche, no. I don't want her riding past the cliff at night."

"All right, then, first thing in the morning. Let him know what happened and he'll figure out what to bring. Mr. Callahan will be just fine here with me."

Becca was unsure what to do. Leaving Jared with Mrs. Cain seemed most unseemly. What had Fletcher said about her? "Jared?"

"Jared?" Mrs. Cain asked. "You let the help call you Jared?"

"Blanche, she isn't the help. I'd like for you to meet my wife, Becca Callahan."

Becca had pitched hay a time or two since she'd been here and she'd brushed the horses, but she hated to admit she hadn't yet caught on to milking the cow. Well, she'd have to learn in short order. Long hours into the evening, she finished the chores. And she'd given Charger an extra measure of oats and an apple for all his hard work during the day, but her mind never drifted from Jared, not for one second.

*I'd like to know who she thinks she is. Much too friendly with* my *husband, if you ask me.*

She patted the cow's rump. "Sorry, girl, didn't mean to take my anger out on you. But that woman has no right. Just because they've been friends forever. Or maybe. Maybe they were more than friends. Still are." She rose from her work and leaned against the solid rump, her eyes brimming with tears. What did she expect?

After all, she had made it clear she'd married Jared in name only. Just to have a home. Hadn't the Cain woman seen through them? She recognized Becca was nothing more than the hired help. If she recognized that, then so would the entire town.

Star kicked at the bucket, nearly upending it, and Becca jumped out of the way. When she bawled a second time, Becca figured she should finish and go in for the night. "Better get used to me, girl. It'll be you and me for quite a while. That man's hurt himself good."

Creamy, frothy milk filled the other pail. Becca, rather pleased with herself, lugged them to the house to go down to the cellar. Jared always strained the milk first, but exhaustion closed in on her like a cloak in winter.

Back in the kitchen, shadows danced on the walls, sending her first to one corner and then the other looking for hoodlums and bandits. She washed, pulled her nightgown over her head and tugged a shawl around her shoulders, but still had a bad case of the frights. Finally she understood just how safe Jared made her feel. How comfortable his presence was beside her. Not as a friend or a boss, but as a protector. He made her feel safe.

On bare feet, she crossed over the cold boards. She entered his room and lifted his nightshirt from the end of the four-poster. Drawing in a deep breath, she imagined him standing here, reaching out his arms for her. The shirt smelled of so many comforting things, but mostly of Jared. The soapy goodness and the musky smell of hard work that was all him.

Hiking her leg up, she struggled into the big bed, where she scrunched the shirt in her hands and placed it under her head. It didn't take long for her eyes to begin to droop with contentment.

Jared guzzled the cup of water Blanche held in her hand. He'd already started to feel much better after the hot soup and having his wound cleaned and the bleeding stopped. "Blanche, what was that sidewinder, Fletcher, doing out here this morning? Gave Becca some story that I know to be untrue."

She tucked the poultice tight around the wound. "Huntin' for some girl named Jesse. Now, I'm a saloon keeper's daughter, Jared. Not some dummy. Even if I knew where to find that girl, no way would I tell a bad apple like him. That whole bunch who bought the saloon after Pa died? Why, I wouldn't give you one red cent for any of 'em. But Fletcher's the worst. He preys on young girls to work for him. I pray that Jesse girl got away."

He shifted against the pillow. "I don't recall him being from around here."

"He came out several months ago. Right after Bart died. He brought three more girls to work the saloon.

I don't like it. No, sir. And Bobby doesn't take to him, either. Sheriff better do more than look the other way or our town's going to fall apart. Don't trust Fletcher, Jared. Not for one minute. When my daddy ran the saloon, it was on the up-and-up. No dishonest gambling. No messing around with the girls. They were treated right and you know it. A man came in for a cool drink and a song or two and went on his way. No funny business."

"So he's branching out."

"Seems like it." Her fingers fluttered over the torn strips of sheet as she wound them snug about his leg. He did his best not to cry out. "Travels back and forth a lot, and he spends a lot a' time tryin' to look respectable and all. But I see him for the snake he is." She scrunched the pillow behind Jared's head. "I wouldn't trust him as far as… Well, you could spit."

Jared smiled. "You're quite a girl, Blanche."

She elbowed his side. "Go on, now. I'm no girl anymore. But I guess I've still got a lot of life left in me. I thought… Well, doesn't matter now, does it?"

He patted her hand and smiled. Bart had been his best friend. No way could he have even considered courting Blanche after Bart was gone. "You're a treasure, Blanche. Good a friend as your husband was to me." He jerked, his leg blazing like hot embers. "Careful there. That hurts!"

"Oh, don't be a baby." She finished dressing the wound. "Anyway, you keep that pretty wife away from Fletcher. He's no good, Jared. And I know. I can see a bad one from thirty paces. Daddy taught me. He's up to no good."

Jared lifted himself on his elbow. "She can't stay at the ranch alone."

"What? Who?"

"Becca. She won't be safe without me there."

"You sure you married that girl? I thought they said in town she's just a hired hand. I'm surprised at you, Jared."

"We're married. We just... Well, she didn't have anywhere to go. She's going to help with the ranch. I'm going to—"

"That true?" Blanche threw back her head and belly-laughed most unladylike. "Well, will you look at that? Clacinda Sherwood couldn't catch you, but that little slip of a girl did. Some sad story, huh? That's a doozy and one Bart would really egg you on about. So she's a bride for your convenience. Or maybe it's more for hers." Blanche didn't make any attempt to try to hide her amusement for his sake at all. "Well, if the way she worried herself over you tonight was any indication, she's not gonna stay the hired help for long. You need you a good woman. If it can't be... You just take care of yourself, you hear?"

He cringed and knew his face must be a dozen different shades of red. Better not say what he wanted; he'd just dig himself deeper.

"You done bandaging my leg and laughing at me?"

"I'm done bandaging, but I'm not about to make any other promises."

"Can you at least help me onto a horse? I'll bring it back in a day or two. But I need to go home."

She patted his arm. "Let's not be fooli—"

"Blanche, I'm headin' out. Whether you help me or leave me here, I intend to get home tonight."

She was still laughing, tears threatening her eyes. "I'll hook up the buckboard again. You're more love-sick than that mangy old horse of yours. Why, I never."

Jared cleared his throat in an effort to stop her ramblings. "No, I wouldn't want you riding back alone. Not with that no-good Fletcher around. I'll be fine. Just help me get saddled."

"You sure?"

"Well, if I'm not, you'll discover a sorry carcass surrounded by buzzards tomorrow morning."

"You're sorry, all right. And I don't know of a buzzard hungry enough to settle on you." She leaned in and grinned. "Let me saddle Strawberry for you. No need for you to kill yourself before you get home. You'll be lucky if she gets there by next week."

Jared read something in her eyes. Loneliness? Had she really thought they might get together? Well, she'd kept it to herself long enough. But no, her husband had been his good friend. He'd never have considered courting her even after a respectable amount of time; best friends didn't do that to each other.

Barely able to prevent his head from falling onto the horse's mane, Jared, at last, made out the house through the darkness. He'd have to see to the horse before he could head in. But he managed with a bit of effort. Blanche had given him a wooden crutch of sorts to lean on and he shuffled his way to the house as quietly as possible. Without a lamp, all was dark as could be. But he noticed Becca's fichu, bloodied and torn, on the hat rack by the front door. At least she'd made it home safe. Thank God. Then she'd no doubt fallen into bed, exhausted and emotionally drained.

He smelled a pot of coffee still on the stove but couldn't bring himself to pour a cup. Instead, he headed straight for bed.

He opened the door, stepped inside. A groan escaped his lips, and he set the crutch firmer against the floor to carry his weight, all the while trying not to awaken Becca in the next room. With the injured ribs, his breathing had become ragged. He stopped. Sweat covered his face. Blanche had been right; he shouldn't have made the trip home.

In the morning, he'd talk to Becca, thank her for all she'd done, including leaving him warm coffee. Now, that was a wifely thing to have done. He smiled.

He struggled to the bed. No need to change out of his clothes. As tired as he felt, he wasn't sure he could maneuver out of them even if he had the inclination. Not sure he'd make it into the high bed, he grasped the edge of the end post and hauled himself up very carefully, then landed with a thunk.

Screams pierced his eardrum.

Becca flailed her arms over her head. "Let go of me! Let go! Get away! Help!"

"Becca. Shhh. What are doing in here? Are you all right?"

She slapped in the direction of the familiar voice. Warm arms encircled her, forcing her to remain still and listen. "It's me, Jared. Why are you in my room?"

"What?" She jerked away from the warm cocoon, rubbing sleep from her eyes. "Jared?" Scrunching her nightgown in her fingers, she fought for words, but nothing seemed to come to mind. "I—uh. Well, I… You see…"

"No, Becca. I don't see and I certainly didn't mean to frighten you."

She slid over the edge of the high four-poster and turned away from his voice. "There were noises and… Well, I was afraid. They were coming from the front and I thought I might not be as scared in here with Cromwell to keep me company."

Should she merely climb back in bed and draw from his strength? His warmth? What would he think of her? Forward, no doubt. After all, they were only friends. But perhaps he wouldn't mind so much. She was more afraid now than she had been when she thought she was alone.

"Jared? How did you get home?" She must be dreaming, but his arms had been real enough, safe enough.

"Blanche saddled Strawberry for me."

"Strawberry?"

"Becca, can we talk in the morning? I'm so tired and every bone in my body screams for sleep. I suppose I should have stayed at Blanche's. Now my leg is on fire."

"Why didn't you?"

"Didn't I what?"

"Why didn't you stay there?" He could barely move when she'd left him. Didn't he know he was taking his life in his hands coming all this way?

"I was worried about—"

"About me?" *Oh, please let him have been concerned for me. That way I'll know he cares.* "Jared?"

The only sound from the big bed was a soft snoring.

Becca tucked the covers firmly around Jared and with a heavy heart shifted on her heels for her own room.

If Jared hadn't pretended to be asleep, he would have pulled her into his arms and stopped all this nonsense, but he'd made a pledge. Until she remembered who she was or decided that she truly wanted to be his wife, they wouldn't share a room. *Lord, what kind of promise was that? What was I thinking? She isn't a servant. She's my wife!*

He wiped sweat from his face, tugged the covers over his shoulder and tried to place his leg in a comfortable position. There wasn't one. Just like his life. Uncomfortable in every sense of the word. Forget Becca for a moment. He should probably get up and soak the wound on his leg, but the comfortable bed was calling him to sleep. Maybe by morning… No. Time to succumb to his exhaustion. What a horrible day, and if it hadn't been for Becca, he wouldn't ever have seen another. She'd saved his life.

With a groan that surely had been heard all the way to town, he closed his eyes and prayed for blessed sleep, but all he pictured was beautiful blond curls and eyes bluer than a clear lake on a hot summer day. *Jared, you're a dreamer. You've always been a dreamer. This accident should wake you up to what your life is going to be from here on out.*

# Chapter 9

A cool rag soothed Jared's forehead, pulling him from sleep. Opening his eyes, he watched as Becca wrung the cloth and bathed his face again. "Thank you. Feels so good."

Her face still held the fearful expression she had worn the evening before, and it was all his fault. He'd caused her worry by coming home when she already had enough to be concerned with on the ranch.

"You're burning up this morning. I'll be going to town for the doctor."

He struggled to his elbow. "Let me saddle—"

"No. If Mrs. Cain can do it, I can do it. I've been watching you saddle the horses. I know how. I'll be back as soon as possible. Keep this on your head. You're terribly hot, Jared. Why did you come home last night? You should have stayed put, you know."

He fell back against the pillows and stared at the ceiling. "I was afraid for you, Becca. That Fletcher fella's been nosing around hereabouts. Blanche told me he was out bothering her yesterday. I was afraid he might come back."

"Oh, Jared." Her words were filled with compassion. If only she would wrap her arms around his neck and bury her face in his chest. He longed to show her how much he cared, but she kept to herself, her hands at her sides, the stoic little soldier who didn't care to share her emotions with him. Or maybe she truly didn't feel anything for him. How was he to know?

"Take Strawberry. She's gentle like Tinker. Besides, Charger might still be shy after the snake."

"All right."

Her fingers brushed his hot skin and the soft touch reached deep into his belly. If only she'd stay. He wouldn't need a doctor. He wouldn't need anything else in the world. "Thank you, Becca. For everything. I owe you my life." Needing rest more than wishes, he allowed himself to slip deeper into the comfort of the feather pillow.

After more than a dozen attempts to saddle Strawberry, Becca finally managed to ride into town in record time. She slid off Strawberry's back and dashed into Dr. Parker's office. "You need to come right away. He's hurt bad. Please, Dr. Parker."

"Whoa. Hold on there. What happened? Who's hurt?"

"Jared! Who else?" She spent the next few minutes explaining and then trying to make excuses for Jared riding back home in such a condition. Embarrassed that he had risked his life, she mumbled and scrambled for explanations.

In a matter of minutes they were in the doctor's buggy riding for home, Strawberry tethered to the back.

"You think it's broken?" Parker asked.

"I'm not sure of anything. I only know he said Charger shied from a snake, threw him and landed on his ankle. There was a rock under it. Mrs. Cain didn't think there was a break, but he lost a lot of blood. The wound runs the length of his leg. I'm afraid of infection. And as if that's not enough, he was holding his side. Said it's hard to breathe because his ribs hurt so."

Dr. Parker shook his head. "Sounds nasty. We'll see what can be done. As soon as we arrive, you start grating potatoes."

Becca drew her chin in. Hardly a time to be thinking of Jared's stomach. She doubted he'd have much appetite anyway in his condition, but then again, men knew each other better than she did. "Potatoes?"

"We'll make a poultice. Hopefully a good poultice will prevent an infection. But if there already is one, nothing draws it out like shredded potato. We'll alternate potato and brown sugar."

She stared ahead, trying to make sense of his words. Potatoes. "Whatever you say. I want to help. I'll do anything you ask, Dr. Parker."

The doctor turned his head. "And how are you, young lady? Wasn't but a few weeks ago that I treated you for a bump on the head. Any chance your memory's come back?"

"I'm fine. A headache now and then, but the bruise is gone and, well…as for my memory, not much. I could be the First Lady of the United States and I wouldn't know it unless I attended some fancy dinner with the president."

"Hmm. Good thing Jared knew who you were, isn't it? Must be frightening not knowing where you're from. I suppose you're adjusting to married life by now."

What could she say? *No, we aren't really husband and wife? He works the ranch, I'm a—what had Mrs. Cain called her—hired girl?* She had no right to be angry about that, either. She was, after all, just a servant on the ranch. Her choice as much as his.

"We're getting on." But from the sound of it, he was getting on with that Blanche Cain more. Just what were they to each other?

He eyed her from under a crooked eyebrow as if he discerned their secret. "Getting on. Now, that's a fine how-do-you-do. Not even a newlywed blush for the doc?"

That question certainly brought one. Becca put a hand on her face and turned her head to the side. He seemed to read her very thoughts, and if he continued to look into her eyes he'd surely realize the truth. Dread slithered through her veins like that snake under Charger's hooves. And scared her as much. She couldn't allow folks in town to gossip. Not about her and Jared. He was too good a man to have folks whispering. "Dr. Parker, Jared was running a fever when I left. We should get there quick." She eyed him from the side.

With one last raise of his eyebrow, Dr. Parker slapped the reins and hurried them along without another word.

The rag, no longer cool, fell to the side of Jared's head. And he didn't have enough strength to shake it out and put the thing back. Had she gone for the doc yet? He struggled to sit up but the pain in his leg and ribs shocked him back against the bed. At last, he took a deep breath and tugged the covers away so he could survey the purple stain surrounding his ankle. The depth of the jagged cut worried him. Worse than he'd thought, but better than it might have been. His sister had taught him to always look on the bright side. And he would.

Blanche had cleaned it well, and even if there was an infection, Doc would know what to do to make it better. Hadn't he seen to Tinker's leg when she was hurt? Well, Doc might be able to mend his leg, but he'd never be able to mend his heart. All of his hopes and dreams had died the day the train derailed. No wife, merely a hired hand with a lovely shape and face who didn't know her own name, let alone his when she'd arrived.

Pulling the quilt back over his leg, he stretched out and a moan escaped him. Why was the room so hot? He closed his eyes and allowed the warmth to draw him back to sleep.

Becca pressed Dr. Parker through the door. The hot smell of sickness filled her nostrils. "In here. He's in here." She pointed to the bedroom in the back of the house.

Her gaze ran alongside the doctor's as they walked past the spare room. The bed, mussed and unkempt, showed through the open door. Maybe he'd think she slept in the front room so Jared's leg wouldn't be jarred.

He cleared his throat. "If you'd be kind enough to boil some water and bring me clean rags, I'll be cleaning this wound out." The doc's hands pressed onto Jared's brow and he shook his head. "The boy's hot."

"Is he..." She twisted her fingers until they hurt. "Is he going to be all right?"

"We'll just see what we see, young lady. I haven't even had a chance to examine him. Run along and fetch the rags."

She stayed in the doorway, not wanting to leave Jared. This wasn't fair—Jared was hurt and maybe dying. Her coming had created so many problems for this good man. She should have gone back. To where? If she was Rebecca Layne, it wasn't much of a life to return to. And if she wasn't Miss Layne, then where might she end up without Jared's protection?

"Hop to it, girl. I need boiled water, clean rags or a sheet torn into strips and plenty of shredded potatoes. Are you going to help?"

"Sorry." She dashed from the doorway immediately.

Her mind offered no peace. This was all her fault. If he'd married that Sherwood girl or even his beautiful widowed neighbor, he'd be happy now. Not living a life of lies. Becca was a terrible wife. She should have gone looking for him as soon as he was late to dinner. You could set your clock by the man's stomach. A good wife would have understood that, wouldn't she?

She plopped the fresh kettle on the stove and grabbed clean clothes from the basket in the corner. These should have been put away. She heaved a sigh. She wasn't even a good hired girl. Jared deserved better. A better wife, better housekeeper, better helpmate.

Dr. Parker's voice floated into the room. "Let's go, young lady. I need to clean this wound."

Becca grabbed the wooden handle and dragged the basket along with her. "Here you go. How does his leg look?"

"Mean and nasty as a rattler. But I believe he'll be all right if we can get the fever down. I've seen a whole lot worse. Come over here and I'll show you how to wash around the wound and change the dressing. Every couple hours, mind you. And keep him warm. We wanna sweat this fever out. Make tea out of the elder flowers I gave you."

"Flowers?"

He handed her a small bag. "You're going to make tea out of it and give him a cup every couple hours. It will help him sweat it out. He needs the fluids, and the tea will help. Alternate that with plenty of cool water. Whatever you have to do, however, keep the boy warm." He aimed a stare her way. "Got those potatoes grated?"

"No." Becca hurried from the room. She scrubbed two fat potatoes, cleaned them well and began to grate. Was she supposed to pat them dry or keep the shavings damp? She certainly didn't know much about home remedies. You'd think Dr. Parker would have some new miracle to help Jared. Potatoes and flower tea, indeed. Doctors were supposed to know everything.

At last, she placed them in a clean cloth and dashed to the bedroom. "Here you go."

Dr. Parker dipped the cloth in the scalding water, wrung it out, potatoes and all, and placed it over the wound. He tied another piece of cloth over the top, pulling it tight.

Jared groaned as his leg twitched beneath the hot poultice. Then, almost immediately, he shook from the top of his head to the balls of his feet. Chills.

"Is he going to be all right?"

"Patience." The doctor stared at her over the top of his glasses. "Time'll tell."

She chewed the edge of her lip. "Shouldn't you splint his ankle?"

"What do you know about splinting?"

"I'm not sure. But I believe I've seen this kind of wound before."

"Well, you're right. Once you've soaked that wound for a full day, I intend to put a board alongside the leg. I don't want him moving it around much until the tissue's had a chance to heal some." He pulled a thin wooden strip from his bag. "I'll also bring a proper set of crutches later today. He isn't to think about getting out of bed for at least a week. I don't want any weight on that leg."

"He'll stay here if I have to tie him down." She removed the cloth and waited for further instructions. She eyed the chamber pot just under the edge of the bed. Her face flamed. But she would do what was necessary to keep him in bed. She'd care for Jared, the ranch and anything else that needed tending to.

Jared tried to turn over; Becca pushed him back into the thick softness of the feather tick. "Jared, don't move around so much."

Dr. Parker took the cloth and squeezed fresh hot water through it. "And take it easy on those ribs. I've got you bound up real tight, but moving around a lot is going to be painful. One's broken, a couple bruised real bad. You'll be all right." He stood back, eyed the man in the bed and shook his head.

Jared wheezed through tight lips, "My leg?"

"Tonight will tell about that leg. I'll come back in the afternoon, but you, missy, just keep changing the poultices. Use fresh gratings every third or fourth time. Do you have enough potatoes on hand?"

"We do. Jared recently bought supplies for me."

Dr. Parker walked toward the door. "Remember, I don't want him to be chilled. Keep him warm at all costs. This needs to sweat out. If the elder flower tea doesn't work, try the willow bark. Same thing—make a good hot tea and get him to drink it every couple of hours. One or the other will eventually bring the fever down. If you don't see an improvement after the first few cups, switch to the other." He latched his bag and stopped for a second. His pensive gaze troubled Becca.

"What is it, Dr. Parker?"

"You, young lady. Listen, your hands are going to be full. I'll talk with Jared's worker, Cutcher's boy, let him know there'll be extra duties for a while. Then I intend to bring my niece out later today. You have the chores and plenty of the work here on the ranch. She can keep an eye on Jared for you while you go about your business. She's tended to a good many of my patients in the past."

"Your niece?"

"Yes. Not sure if you met her or not. Her name's Clacinda Sherwood. We just call her Clancy."

# Chapter 10

Teeth chattering till he thought they'd clatter right out of his head, Jared moaned, "So cold." A heaviness covered him and he kicked at it. Pain ricocheted through his leg. Trapped. He was trapped in a small space and couldn't get out. He kicked again at his restraints.

Then Charger leaped into the air and came crashing down on him. He groaned.

"Jared? Can you hear me? Don't kick the quilts. That's why you're cold. You need to keep covered. Please. I want you to get well."

*What happened to Charger? Where am I? Home. Becca wants me well.* If he died, she would inherit the entire ranch. A future. A life without him. Maybe she'd be happy. He squeezed his eyes shut. "Becca?"

"Yes?" Her hands tucked and poked the heaviness closer to him. Her face. A look of sadness crowded her brow. Could it be she cared what happened to him?

He squinted to see her better through grainy, tired eyes. "The rest of the letters. In the drawer." He lifted his hand to point, but his arm fell like heavy lead. He licked dry lips. "The top drawer. The rest of the letters from you."

"I don't need to read a bunch of silly old letters. You need sleep, Jared. Close your ey—"

"Please." He needed to stand up. Get to the barn. Take care of the chores. His horses had to be let out to run. "Will you help me get up?"

She placed her hand on his chest, her fingers cold as ice, but they kept him from rising. "Jared. Your leg is badly infected. You should be quiet and sleep to get your strength back. I took care of the animals this morning. You stop worrying."

He pointed again, though it was more difficult this time than the last. "The letters. Read them!"

Becca stumbled into the bedroom, arms loaded with clean, fresh cloths. He'd kicked the covers off again. But he slept at last. She rearranged the quilt, tucking it around his shoulders to stop his shivering.

When finished, she took the cloths to her room, where she folded them into neat stacks ready to be used as bandages. All the while she eyed the dresser against the wall. Foolishness and nonsense. There was too much to be done to worry about those horrible letters. And besides, what difference did it make whether she read them or not? She didn't remember a single thing. The letters might as well have been written in Chinese.

Becca wandered into the kitchen to grate more potatoes. Perhaps if he never found out how sure she felt that she wasn't Rebecca Layne, maybe, in time, he would fall in love with Becca. When he looked at her with those big brown eyes, he'd see her, Becca, instead of the girl who wrote the letters, and there would be a chance for them as husband and wife.

Dreams. Nothing but foolish dreams. He was in love with Rebecca Layne, the mysterious woman who had written numerous letters on delicate stationery sprinkled with lilac water. Not a girl without a past. Or perhaps, even worse, she might be a woman *with* a past. He needed someone like Clacinda Sherwood or Blanche Cain. A woman he shared this type of life with, a woman who knew her place…and who she was. She swiped a tear off her cheek and finished grating.

She returned to the bedroom with a fresh poultice. Lifting the quilt and tugging the stale cloth off gently, she felt her stomach lurch. A loud rap on the door pulled her away from the ghastly sight. "Coming." Becca covered his leg, put the poultice in the basin and marched to the door. "I'm coming! Give me a minute."

"Sorry, we thought you might be sleeping." Dr. Parker pushed past her, his arms loaded with packages. "How's he doing? I brought more potatoes and another package of willow root."

"I was just changing the poultice again. Not much change. He's still burning up. Only had a few drops of soup for lunch."

She turned and welcomed Clacinda Sherwood, who Becca couldn't help noticing had a small satchel with her. This woman intended to stay with them. Oh no. "Dr. Parker, about—"

"Mrs. Callahan, my niece has offered to stay right here. At least until Jared is past the most dangerous time. Do you think you could find her a room to stay in until Jared is better? It would save me driving her back and forth each day."

They were both being so kind. She had to be hospitable. Becca sighed. "Of course. Set your things here for now. I'll make up the front bedroom for you." And where would *she* sleep? She thought of the heavy quilt in storage. She might make up a bed on the floor in Jared's room. While the doc and his niece tended to Jared, Becca cleared the front bedroom of her nightgown as discreetly as possible. She put Clacinda's satchel under the vanity and strolled to the kitchen to make tea. Once the niece was settled, she would go out to the barn to tackle the chores.

Entering the back bedroom with tea, Becca heard Clacinda's grating voice. "Say there, cowboy. How did you manage to get yourself into this mess?"

Dr. Parker turned. "Here, let me help you with that tray. Thank you so much for the tea, Mrs. Callahan. Is this one the tea for Jared?"

"Yes, I'm trying the willow bark you gave me. The elder flowers didn't seem to bring down the fever. And please, call me Becca. The Mrs. still has a strange twang to it."

Clacinda looked over her shoulder. "I'll just bet it does." She laid her hand much too close to Jared's chest. "How long have you two known each other?"

Becca stumbled back. As if it were any of *her* business! "Long enough, Miss Sherwood. Long enough."

Dr. Parker poured himself a cup of tea, oblivious of the two women. Becca would like for him to take his niece right back home, but in all honestly, she really did need the help. "Miss Sherwood, thank you for coming all the way out here, but I'm sure I'll manage just fine. I can always call on Mrs. Cain if I need help."

Clacinda shook her head. "I wouldn't think of it. You're new in town and it's up to all of us to make you feel welcome. If I can help in any way, well, then, that's my contribution." She offered a too-familiar look at Jared before continuing. "Jared and I have been friends for years. It's my pleasure to be of service to you both."

Becca understood insincerity when she heard it. Clacinda Sherwood had made her intentions clear. Becca would not trust the woman. And to think, she had been worried about Blanche Cain. Would it always be like this? Worrying about Jared with other women? With his handsome features and kindness, he must have had quite the life before she came to the ranch. How many women? How many looks would come her way? She had to stop the nonsense. Jealousy didn't become any woman…or man, for that matter.

Dr. Parker finished his tea, took one last glance toward Jared and let himself out of the room. He gestured for Becca to accompany him. "The worst time will be just before the fever breaks. Keep the cold washcloths for his head, hot poultices for his leg. Don't hesitate to let Clancy assist you. She knows a good deal about doctoring. I trust her. You should, too." He held his finger aside his nose. "And, young lady, while she can be brusque, she has good intentions. You needn't worry about Clancy and your husband. No matter how she might wish things were different, Jared has made it abundantly clear to her right from the start that they are merely friends." He patted her arm. "No green-eyed monster, now. He's your husband. Don't you forget that."

He had heard his niece's insinuation? Her face

flamed hotter than a stove poker. "I'm sure I don't know what you are talking about."

He clipped her under the chin. "Sure you don't. Your husband is safe in Clancy's hands. I promise you. And I spoke with that young man who helps your husband now and again, Jeremy Cutcher. He said he'd be around right away. Said he'd handle the trees and fields if you could take care of the animals. Not to worry, he's a serious young man."

"Thank you."

"If any other problems should arise, send Clancy into town to get me. Let her help you, Mrs. Callahan. You look exhausted already. We don't want you collapsing. You need to be the strength for both you and your husband for a while."

Becca blushed and grabbed her shawl from the doorway. She followed him out of the house. She might as well head straight for the barn and get the chores finished. She hadn't given the calf her share of the milk yet. A wave of her hand and she sent the doctor on his way.

With the last of the chores tended to, at least for now, Becca figured she should start supper. When she stepped into the kitchen, Clancy had the dinner soup reheating on the back of the stove. "There's coffee, fresh and hot, if you'd like some." Clancy set a cup on the table next to the sugar. "I'm sorry if I overstepped my bounds today. You see, I always thought… Well, it doesn't matter now. I am sorry. All I want to do is to make you comfortable with my being here. You'll find me helpful and perhaps even find me a friend… one day." She poured coffee into the cup and held it out for Becca. "When you arrived, I thought you were just here to, well, to take Jared's ranch. But he and I talked."

"You what?" As much as she disliked it, Becca took the coffee.

"I can see how you care for him. Seems I had it all wrong. Jared really loves you. He made that real clear." She bit the edge of her lip. "Soup will be ready soon. I hope it's all right that I got started on supper. Maybe we can get that man of yours to eat something."

*That man of mine. I only wish he were mine.* Becca tried on a smile, but she was sure it didn't fit. Was Clacinda sincere? She hadn't seemed so before. Or maybe Becca had read her wrong. What did Jared say to Clacinda while she was out doing chores? "Thank you. For everything, Clacinda."

"I understand you didn't get much sleep last night caring for Jared. Up early to fetch my uncle. If you would like, I can keep watch while you take a nap."

"I would be indebted to you. I'll lie down in the front bedroom." She started to walk away, but turned back. "Thank you, Clacinda."

"Clancy. All my friends call me Clancy."

"Okay, Clancy. Your being here means a lot. To both of us."

Clancy turned back to stir the soup. "I'll wake you at supper time."

Becca stopped. "Do you think I should make a fresh poultice?"

Clancy shooed her from the room. "I think you should get some sleep."

Becca knew sleep wouldn't come easily. She stopped at the dresser by the door and peeked inside the top drawer, where she'd tucked the letters last night. With-

out fanfare, she lifted the papers and drew them to
her bosom. Locked in these pages were secrets. Secrets about a woman she didn't know—a woman she
wanted to get acquainted with. Because even if she
wasn't Rebecca Layne, she longed to understand what
their dreams had been for the future. Maybe Rebecca's
dreams could become hers.

Sitting on the edge of the bed, she drew the next letter into her hands.

> *May 25, 1882*
> *Dear Jared,*
> *Forgive me if that sounds too familiar, but already
> I feel as if I have known you a very long time.*
>
> *Your thoughts are dear to me. I cannot wait for
> the opportunity to meet you. It will feel so strange
> moving from a big city to the country.*

Becca stopped, read and reread the last lines again.
Big city? But didn't she have a neighbor Spencer? She
must have grown up in the country. A city girl would
not likely sew her own clothes, and Becca was certain
she had sewn before.

> *I hope I can accustom myself to the wild beasts
> that live on your ranch. I have to admit to never
> having even seen a cow or pig up close. Only on
> my dinner plate. We don't have so much as an old
> hound dog, so you will have to teach me the ways
> of the country.*

She'd not even seen a farm animal, and no dog? How
could Becca be Rebecca Layne? Perhaps she was read-

ing this incorrectly. Or perhaps Rebecca was simply playing a game with Jared to make him feel important. Oh dear. She hoped not. She didn't want to find out she was such a woman as that.

*I expect my mother will be scandalized when she uncovers my plans, and Father's mother, Grandmother Layne, too. Goodness! Oh well, she will hold me as Mother chastises me soundly. I can count on one friend in all of this, my grandmother Swift.*

But Becca had a grandmother Ellis! And she'd had a dog when she was a child; she was certain of that. Rebecca Layne could…not…be…Becca. What would Jared think if he knew?

*I can't wait to see you, to see my new home. I long to make it my own.*
*Your loving Rebecca*

Had she read wrong? Perhaps this was all a mistake. Her memory might be fooling her; after all, she didn't really know any details about herself. About a past so illusive it might fly away. Maybe the neighbor Spencer or Grandma Ellis came from a book she'd read.

*June 23, 1882*
*Dearest Jared,*
*I apologize for being so remiss in writing. I have been quarreling with my tedious parents. They are insisting I marry a man they have chosen for me. I have not told them about my plans to*

*leave. But I am afraid they suspect something.
They have pressured me a great deal in the past
month. I realize they have my best interests at
heart, but I don't want the same things in life that
they want for me.*

*I am excited to try to live the rustic life. It
all sounds terribly quaint. So that I am not discovered, I shan't write again until I am ready to
leave. Do know that I am anxious to undertake
this trip and make you my loving husband.
Lovingly yours,
Rebecca*

And then she wrote in August that she was arriving
on the train in September. Becca stood, walked to the
dresser and picked up the pen. Now that her hand had
nearly healed, she signed her name. Rebecca Layne.

Nothing at all like the letter writer's signature. Those
memories had not come from a book.

She realized, with all certainty, she was *not* Rebecca
Layne.

Who was talking? And why couldn't he move his
leg? Jared twisted around in the covers. Had he put
too much wood in the fireplace? He could feel the heat
scorching his face. He should get up and put the fire
out, but his leg would not comply.

"He's talking in his sleep."

"Don't bother trying to awaken him. He can eat later.
He's really burning up."

Later? He was hungry now, but who was in his house
and what was burning? Two women's voices. Who were

they? He tried to open his eyes but they pushed into his head and darkness took him again.

A warm hand and a cold cloth awakened him. "Feels good."

"Do you think he's delirious?"

*Who's delirious? Who are they and what poor soul are they discussing?* "Somebody sick?" He forced the lids of his eyes up. Sweat speckled his forehead and dripped down his face.

"Jared, are you awake?"

"Hey, it's…you. Rebecca Layne. No, Becca Callahan. Mrs. Callahan." He fought to speak above a whisper. "Where have you been?" His eyes crossed as his head lifted from the pillow.

Becca jiggled his shoulder, trying to get him to focus on her face. "Hey there. How do you feel?" His eyes narrowed, then he smiled—wide.

She put a hand on his forehead and mirrored his smile. "Cool. Your head is cool at last. Thank You, God."

Clancy stepped quietly from the room, allowing them some time alone. Becca would thank her later; for now, all she wanted was to feel his cool skin under her fingers. It meant he was going to be all right. A tear dribbled over her cheek and she reached up to wipe it away.

Should Becca tell him what she'd discovered? He might send her straight home. No, that wouldn't be possible, because if she wasn't Rebecca Layne, neither of them knew where she came from. But he could send her away, at least.

A shudder coursed through her.

From an obviously dry and scratchy throat, Jared

mumbled, "You all right?" Even with him ill, his protective nature showed his concern. "Why are you... crying?"

Becca grabbed his hand, held it to her chest before she realized how intimate it must appear. Now, more than ever, she had to keep her distance. "Why, I should be asking you that. Feeling better?" She slipped his hand back under the quilt.

"I am now." His eyes lingered on her face, her lips. Her breath hitched in her chest.

She stepped back, out of his reach, and dashed toward the door. "I'll get you some soup, then."

"Becca?"

Her feet continued scurrying away without hesitation. "Be back in a minute with bread and soup. Good to see you looking so much better."

## Chapter 11

Four days after Clacinda vacated their home, Jared wobbled to his feet with the aid of the cane. So glad to be rid of the crutches, he actually looked forward to the chores this morning. He'd missed the comforting smell of the barn and the animals and longed to brush and look after his sleek string of horses. None of them had seen enough exercise in the past few days. And his horses were his life.

Becca's face gave way to her concern. "I still think I should do the chores for a few more days until you're more stable. Jeremy Cutcher said he'd stay on another two weeks. He might not be the most knowledgeable about your horses, but he cares. And he's a hard worker, Jared. He's taken good care of the ranch. Between the two of us, you could get another week or two of rest. Mend that leg. Clancy even offered to stay on and do house chores for me if you thought we needed her."

He leaned heavily on the cane and faced her, stared directly into her eyes with what he hoped would be the final word on the subject. "I realize Jeremy's capable, Becca, but neither of you knows just how to tend to those horses properly. Jeremy does well with the orchard and some of the ranch work, but my animals, as you know, are my responsibility. My ranch depends on the breeding, the feeding, the overall care of my horses. Without a fine herd of animals, this ranch would go under. I have to be the one to make the hard decisions. I appreciate your wanting to help. Truly, I do. But this is my job, and if I have to crawl from stall to stall to see their needs are met, I will."

"But, Jeremy—"

"No." He shook his head. "I have a good ranch, Becca, but my lying around acting like a hound dog that can't hunt isn't helping anyone. And it's uncomfortable for me. Now that I can get around, I'll do fine. I might move a little slower, but moving is what's going to make my leg better. When one of my horses comes up lame, I baby him a bit, and then I get him back on his legs. Exercise, fresh air, good feed, all things that make him better. Well, a man is no different. He needs to move to keep going." He lifted the cane to make his point. "I won't get better unless I push myself the same way I'd push one of my horses. Relying on Jeremy for their care as well as picking the apples will make me lazy, and the only thing that will do is cause me to feel sorry for myself. Not a good combination for a man, Becca. Not at all."

Becca brushed her hands on her apron. "Then I'll put dinner on. Hope you feel like some hot stew with dumplings. And I'll bet I can find time to put together a special dessert, as well."

"Once I'm back from town, that'll hit the spot." He hoped his grin showed his approval. He could live on desserts all the time if he were allowed. He hadn't had many since he'd lived with his sister.

Becca's smile disappeared and her eyes narrowed. "Town?"

He stepped forward, clipped her chin. "Yes, once the chores are done, I'm taking half a dozen chickens to doc as part of my payment. He spent a good deal of time here, and I plan to take chickens to the Sherwoods, as well. I can't in all good conscience do less."

Becca started to speak, must have thought better of it and turned for the kitchen. "You're a stubborn man, Jared Callahan."

He couldn't very well argue with that.

It felt good to be outside. The chores hadn't felt like chores this morning. Not a bit. Now, with a mended Tinker pulling the wagon and the breeze whistling around him, Jared committed himself to the freedom of the moment. He'd planned for this outing to restore his masculinity. For the past two and a half weeks he'd functioned under the assumption he could do nothing for himself. More truth than assumption. Women wiping his face, feeding him. Not the sort of thing that made a man feel much like a man. Might have been different if he and Becca had a real marriage, but without that familiar intimacy, her care of him had been downright humiliating.

Breathing deeply of the countryside, he pushed all other thoughts away. The air was ripe and sweet with the richness of late autumn. All kinds of trees shedding their crops, apples his favorite. He'd make short order of the trip to town just so he could get back for stew and dumplings. His mouth watered and he swallowed hard. Not much had tempted him the past couple of weeks, but his appetite was definitely coming back.

Once life returned to normal, he planned to get Becca a horse of her own so they could ride together. Tinker, too much of a workhorse, only carried a rider so far before balking, and the rest of his horses he already had plans for. Becca would need a sweet little mare, one she could learn to take care of, call her own. And then they could spend evenings riding over their property. The time together might draw them closer.

The squawk of a chicken shifted his attention back to the task at hand, but not for long. Speaking of squawking chickens, why had Becca called in Clacinda Sherwood? Wasn't his embarrassment complete enough with Becca's hovering? A feather flitted across his face. But he couldn't be ungrateful. He would deliver the chickens and bushels of apples Jeremy had picked and be finished with this episode in his life. He supposed he *would* need to keep Jeremy on until all the trees stood empty, but still, he'd do what he could picking from ground level and leave the ladder work to the boy. He laughed to remember Becca grabbing some of the grounders before he could in order to press them into cider. And who knew, maybe he'd square up so well this year he could keep Jeremy on for more than a couple of days a week.

The town came into view ahead. The buildings and boisterous activity hadn't looked this good in a very long time. First, he pulled behind the hotel to deliver the chickens to the Sherwoods, and then he'd swing around to Doc's. Jared felt he owed the doc much more than a few chickens and apples, but Doc liked to barter.

Clacinda stepped onto the porch. "Well, will you look here. What's brought you to town, cowboy?"

He held a small crate aloft with three chickens fluttering and protesting madly. "Thought a few hens might taste mighty good. Or you could keep them for laying. Your pa no doubt could use the fresh eggs." He handed the crate to Clacinda's younger brother, who dashed from the back door to the wagon in record time. "Hey, Toby. Take these to your mama with my best regards."

The boy peeked into the crate, eyes wide and full of mischief. "Aw, can't I play with 'em for a while?"

"No, sir. You get those cacklers to your ma or pa."

In spite of his promise to himself to keep a good distance between them, Jared leaned in Clacinda's direction. "And I thank you kindly for all the help you gave Becca. We both appreciate it. Never realized what a good and kind friend you are, Clacinda."

She blushed from her neck to the roots of her hair. "Anytime, Jared. And when the day comes you need a lady to help Becca with more than that… Oh, fiddlesticks, don't look so prissy. You'd think you were thirteen years old." She pushed the hair from her face. "One day she'll need a midwife and I'll be happy to be of service."

If he'd thought her cheeks had been warm, *his* were downright burning up. Heat, steamy tentacles and all, crept over his skin the way the fever had. He licked his lips and nodded. "Good day." *Come on, Tinker. Get us out of here.*

Giggles erupted behind him. "You remember what I said, now, hear?"

That woman had more gall than a posse of bandits toting six-shooters.

Giving Tinker a handful of oats from the back of the wagon, Jared rubbed her neck and told her she wouldn't have to stand and wait long this time. "I'll give these to the doc and make a quick visit to Mr. Henderson at the post office." He leaned in close. "Be right back, girl." Then he walked around back and slapped her rump. Lifting the chickens out of the wagon, he stared at the shingle. Dr. Parker, Human and Animal Ailments. Which one was he? He hadn't felt much human the past couple weeks.

"Jared, my boy. What are you doing out of bed? Is Becca all right?"

"She's fine. Why do you ask?"

"Well, what are you doing in town? Didn't I tell you just four days ago that you were to take it easy?"

"You did, sir. And I am. I took my time this morning with the chores and—"

"The chores?"

"Now you sound like my wife. I needed to get back to livin', Doc. Lying around makes a man feel useless."

Dr. Parker nodded. "I s'pose." He looked past Jared to the crate on the ground. "What have you got there?"

The doctor hadn't wanted to accept the noisy chickens or the apples, but he gave in at last. It made Jared feel better to pay up. "See here. If you take the chickens and apples, that way you won't be coming out trying to take my ranch in payment for all your hard work."

He slapped Jared's back and reminded him to take it easy for a while.

Now, with the doc all paid up, Jared could mosey

over to the general store and pick up any mail, maybe the new seed catalog for next year that he'd been waiting on, and skedaddle on home before Becca had a chance to worry.

Mr. Henderson laughed when he saw Jared. "Two things for ya, young fella. The seed catalog you been askin' for and a letter." He raised an eyebrow.

Jared frowned. "Letter?" He grasped the two pieces, and if it hadn't been for his sore leg, he'd have run from the office like a house afire.

"Say, young fella, don't forget I'll have a good supply of them seeds in the store come spring. You don't need to order all of 'em. Have a good day. Say hey to that new young wife of yours."

He waved. A letter? From Rebecca? How could that be? Maybe she'd sent another one before she left and she beat it here.

Not likely. She'd been here for weeks. Could a letter take that long to get where it was supposed to go? Maybe it got lost in the mail....

Jared dived into the wagon seat and tore the envelope open.

*October 28, 1882*
*Dear Mr. Callahan,*

Dear Mr. Callahan? What kind of greeting was that from an engaged woman? Was he completely losing his mind?

*I suppose by now you are so angry that I didn't arrive on the train...*

The paper fluttered through his fingers. Didn't arrive? But he was living with Rebecca. She was his wife.

He reached to the floor of the wagon and picked up the paper.

*...nothing I say will bring any comfort. I am so sorry for the way I have treated you. But you see, my family finally convinced me that staying in the city and marrying Parnell Robertson III was the best for all of us. You included, because I would not have made a very good country wife. One visit to my cousin's farm in late June assured me this was the right thing to do. When I heard a hog squeal early in the morning, it nearly made me ill. The thought of butchering time would come to mind whenever I prepared dinner. I guess I wasn't exactly thinking clearly when I made the decision to go out West.*

*I am ever grateful my parents insisted on my visiting Sissy before making any other plans about my future. I think they may have suspected all along, that or my sister let go of her promise and divulged my plans. Either way, I can assure you heading West would have been the worst disaster of my life. And yours. For the thought of being without new gowns and parties to which I could wear them became unbearable.*

*Perhaps a girl can never remove the city from her heart.*

*I can only imagine how you must have felt waiting at the train for a young girl who had neither the courage nor the strength to run away from home. But neither did I have the courage to*

*write you. As shameful as my actions have been,
I simply could not put words to paper. Not until
now. I have discussed this at length with my sister,
who said I was being an uncaring oaf and should
write you immediately.*

*Please accept my heartfelt apology for lacking
in good manners.*

*I wish you the very best in your life. I could not
have been the person to make you happy. I am to
marry Parnell at the height of the Christmas season. Oh, what a wonderful party we shall have.
God bless you,
Miss Rebecca Layne*

He swallowed over a walnut-size lump in his throat.
Miss Rebecca Layne. How very formal from one who
would once have called him her darling. Her love. Now
he felt as if he had lost her not once, but two times. And
to think, all she could say in the end was *Oh, what a
wonderful party we shall have.*

Then who was Becca Callahan? And where had she
come from? If he pressed her any further, she might
not ever remember. But how could they go on living
together? Did she guess she wasn't Rebecca? Was that
why she wanted to be called Becca? The possibility
remained: she might have a family of her own somewhere, waiting for their darling to come home. Maybe
even a husband…

Somehow, they had to find out who she was. If
she was married, he would have to give her up. That
thought sent a pain right through his heart. But surely
she wouldn't have been traveling alone if she was married. And she didn't wear a ring. No, there was hope.

Jared leaned his elbow onto his good thigh and cradled his head in his hand. He had but one choice. Return home and pretend he hadn't received the letter. Somehow he had to make a go of winning Becca over, because if truth be told, he had fallen for her. Hard.

With Jared gone for the morning, Becca stared at the stack of letters—again. Pen in hand, she tried one last time to sign her name with the same flourish as on the letters. It was no use. She could not be Rebecca Layne. Everything in her screamed at the implausibility. Nothing about the signature stood out as remotely similar. And Becca was carefree, wasn't she? This woman sounded like a snob. Becca wasn't a snob...at least, she didn't think so.

Continuing to live here would create all sorts of scandal, if not with Jared's friends, at least in her heart. She was married under false pretenses. She had to leave. His love was out there, somewhere. And they belonged to each other. Until she managed to think of a way to escape without upsetting Jared, this would have to be her home. And this room, her room. But his eyes, the way they looked her over. Warmth crept over her cheeks— again. So often lately, she felt the blush of the new love she couldn't have until she knew for sure where she'd come from. Besides, he belonged to someone else. He loved Rebecca Layne.

The sudden smell of burning food brought her to the kitchen. The edge of the pot had caught. She poured the stew into a smaller cast-iron kettle and set it back from the heat. Just enough to keep the delicious meat and vegetables warm without any more scorching.

*Lord, what should I do? I feel like this stew, as if I'm*

*getting burned merely by being where I shouldn't. Do I have somewhere else to go?*

The sound of wagon wheels outside sent her into a flurry of action. She lifted the cover off the fresh biscuits, which she'd decided to do instead of dumplings, and placed a butter ball on the table next to the basket. A small dish of honey came next. Then she ladled up bowls of stew and poured him a hot cup of coffee. Sitting at the table with her hands in her lap, she waited.

What words would make sense of this? Should he even bring up the subject? Perhaps the less said the better. If Becca honestly did not know who she was, perhaps they could make a life together. They were married, after all. He shook his head as he unhitched the wagon. No, not really. They were a hired girl and her boss. He knew nothing about her. Where she came from. Who her family was. Nothing. Nothing but those sad blue eyes that made him feel as if he owed her his protection. Yet she had been the one to take care of him recently.

A groan issued from his throat. No, a growl, like a gruff old bear. He felt like a bear caught in a trap. His fingers reached up and riffled through his hair. He was so mixed up; he wanted to stay in the wagon and keep driving to the end of the horizon, but he couldn't do that. Instead, he stuffed the letter in his pocket and finished settling Tinker. "Here you go, girl." He heaped hay into her manger but managed to find an apple as a treat for her hard work in spite of the still-tender leg. "You feeling better, old girl? I can honestly say I understand. Nothing like a lame leg to slow a body down. But I'm glad at least you're doing better."

Walking back, his thoughts drifted from the dusty path to the house, his home where Becca, as his wife, would be busily preparing lunch. He swore he could smell the rich, hot coffee being poured and the peppery stew being plated.

Did it matter that there wasn't any past between them? Maybe not, but it sure would make life a whole lot easier if he had something to go by. Something other than a pack of letters that was nothing but dreams...and lies. A pack of letters from another woman altogether.

The noon sun beat down on him and he did his best to hurry in, but his leg slowed him.

Oh, who was he kidding? Feelings were there, at least on his part. When he came home from Blanche Cain's and found Becca in the back room, he had hoped... But no, she said she'd only been lonely. Still, why had she gone to his room?

Women. Who could figure them out? If he hadn't put that foolish ad in the paper in the first place, he would be home right now. Happy. Mending fences, eating on his own time schedule, milking cows, riding Charger across the land. Yes, sirree, happy.

Alone. Too many fences, beans and molasses...again and chores morning and night. Over and over without a break. Cold evenings in the middle of winter that froze not only the feet but the soul. Only church on Sundays offered him a change of pace.

A groan erupted from his chest. He could kid himself only so long. The fact was, he wanted a family. A wife who shared the hard life of work on a ranch. The warm feet to help stave off those cold nights. Children. He longed for a house full of laughing, healthy children to carry on once he was gone. He wanted it all.

Was that so bad? Wasn't that why he'd put the ad in the paper in the first place? He was tired of going it alone. He'd lost his folks and his wonderful sister had filled in, but a sister couldn't be that helpmate to share all of his inner desires. And his best friend's wife was more like a sister, so he'd never given her a thought. Not that way. Blanche was a good soul, but not right for him.

*God, why? I meant the vow when I married Becca. Does she want a real marriage, too?*

*Oh, stop whining, man. If she loved you, really loved you, she'd be by your side.*

Angrily struggling through his pain to get to the house, Jared nearly dropped the package he'd brought. Afraid she might be running low on brown sugar, he'd bought more so he could ask her to make another of those delicious apple pies. If they continued to share the everyday activities, maybe she'd grow comfortable with the arrangement and learn to love him. She certainly didn't now. And why should she? She wasn't Rebecca Layne, after all. And even the real Rebecca Layne wasn't who he'd thought she was.

He had to give Becca the benefit of the doubt. Her life, like his, had been turned topsy-turvy and he had no clue how to put things to right. For now, he would keep the letter to himself. No need for her to be frightened away. If her memory came back, there was time enough to make hard decisions. For the both of them.

"Becca?" he shouted as he entered the front door.

"In the kitchen." Her voice was like soft whispers on the prairie.

Where had that foolish thought come from?

"Wash up, Jared. Dinner's on the table."

## Chapter 12

Becca's fingers trembled as she scooped through the crunchy topping to see if the dish was done. The apples she'd picked this morning were now tangy sweet slices of goodness layered with buttered and browned bread cubes. A light sprinkling of cinnamon accompanied their sugary sweetness. And she'd made a thick caramel sauce to pour over the top. She hoped he'd like it.

She smoothed her apron, tucked a loose curl behind her ear and moved to the table.

"Here you are." Jared offered her a brown-paper package.

"Your food's ready. What's this?" She squeezed the contents without a clue what it contained.

"Thought you might be needing some brown sugar for another of those apple pies. Sure are delicious."

A giggle bubbled from her lips. His eyebrows drooped into a frown. "Did I say something funny?"

"I guess we were thinking the same thing this morning. I picked apples." She spun on her heel and reappeared with the hot, bubbling pan. "Only I baked an apple brown Betty. I think you'll like it every bit as much as pie. It's my specialty." She chewed the edge of her lip. *My specialty. I have a specialty?* Suddenly she pictured an old farm table. Solid, with a linen cloth covering it. A small vase of flowers sat in the middle. No, they were dandelions. And a little girl's fingers were wrapped around it. Curls danced around the child's face. After a second, she let go of the vase and ran her finger through a pan of the apple dessert. Giggling and tasting, she sputtered, "It was the best apples I ever ate."

Becca did have a special treat that she baked...for who? Her daughter?

She set the pan down and lifted her palms to her cheeks. Did Jared notice? How could he not?

"Becca. Are you all right?"

Her hands fluttered from her face. "Certainly. Why not?"

"You looked a little funny."

Air whooshed from her lips. "That's because I had this surprise for you and I was laughing because of the sugar. You see, isn't it funny we both were thinking the same thing? And here I was baking this all along." *Stop rambling. Stop sounding like a fool.* Nervous giggling burst from deep inside.

Then Jared laughed with her. His smile reached from his dimples to the crinkles around his eyes. Handsome as all get out. He was that and more. And when he smiled at her that way, she longed to be a real and true wife. A meaningful part of his life.

Becca moved forward. Tempted to walk right into

his arms, she stopped. Her feet would go no farther. In fact, she thought better of it and stepped back. The laughing ceased, though it hung in the air between them like cool water on a stifling summer day. Had he noticed her nearly step into his arms? She had no right. She wasn't Rebecca Layne. And a dessert didn't change any of that. Not even a specialty.

As she backed away, Jared's hands molded into fists at his sides.

Becca nipped at her lip again. "We'd best go eat before the stew gets cold. Would you grab the coffeepot while I get the sauce for the dessert?"

One minute laughing, the next acting as if he had an old hound dog's fleas. She'd nearly moved into his reach. Jared wasn't that ignorant of women that he couldn't tell when a woman planned to return his affection. Becca had stepped right toward him as his arms came up. She had. Then she'd slipped away just as fast.

The twitching in his heart slowed like his movements lately. Slow and clumsy. She was doing things to him that he didn't like. Distance; there had to be distance between them. More than simply separate rooms. He had to see to it that she didn't crawl any further under his skin or he might not be able to wait for her to walk into his arms; he might grab her and crush her to him without asking. And that would bring nothing but disaster. Now that he knew she wasn't Rebecca, he might force her memories in such a way that she would hate him. Leave him. Forget he'd ever been in her life. The fact was, he was more than a little in love with her. He'd passed that point a long time ago.

Jared slammed the coffeepot on the tablecloth and

sat with a thunk. He eyed the tin pan in the middle of the table. With all the thoughts of Becca swirling in his head, he figured that had better be some wonderful apple brown Betty!

The way Jared spooned in the hot stew nonstop and then the heaping plate of dessert, Becca assumed he'd been starving. She lifted the coffeepot. "Care for some?"

"What? Care for what?"

She hesitated. "Coffee? Would you like some more coffee?"

"I've just had about all the coffee I can stand." He slapped his palm on the edge of the table and stood to his feet. "Good dinner. Thank you, Becca." Suddenly all formal and aloof, his words cut to her heart.

She set the pot back down. "I'm glad you liked it, Jared."

Becca watched him limp away, aware how each step must cost him dearly. But no one would know it. He behaved like a lion on a rampage. What had him all angry and pacing so?

She picked up the empty plates and turned for the kitchen. Over her shoulder, she asked, "Heading out to the barn?"

"No! I still have to mend that fence. Only this time, I'll be ready for any rattlers. Don't expect me back till late. I have a lot to do."

"Shouldn't you take the wagon? Wouldn't that be safer?"

"Becca, I've worked here on my own for years. I don't need a woman telling me what to do."

She put a hand on her face, which burned with shame

for the second time that day. Apparently he had a temper, after all. She'd only suggested. What had him all tied up in knots? Maybe his work was so far behind after his being in bed all this time. She wished she'd have known what to do all along. Maybe she and Jeremy could have fixed that fence and Jared wouldn't feel the need to be doing so much so soon.

Through the fabric of his jeans, Becca noticed how his muscles strained to keep him upright. He shouldn't be out working this hard.

He reached for his hat at the door and stepped out. With a glance over his shoulder, he said, "Remember, I'll be out late. Don't wait up."

The afternoon dragged by even with preparations for supper and then working outside for a while. Becca, wishing she had a friend she could confide in, looked west. Blanche Cain. Jared had assured her they were good friends. His best friend's wife. His widowed wife. Maybe she had room in her life for a good woman friend. That's what Becca needed. Someone she could talk to.

Though the sun no longer hovered straight overhead, she ran for the barn, not even bothering to make herself presentable. Maybe a talk with a friend was just what she needed. She saddled Tinker and thought better of being seen in such disarray. Besides, if she returned to the house, she could wrap up some of the brown Betty for Blanche. Becca would return long before Jared. After all, he said he would be gone till after dark.

With a bag in hand, she struggled to mount Tinker, then let the small mare ease into a trot along the now-familiar path.

Becca must have had friends before. She was an outgoing person. How she longed to sit with a cup of tea and talk over the day's events. With another woman, a confidante. She was not sure how she could tell, but one thing was certain: she knew she missed long conversations with a friend. Blanche had been so helpful when Jared fell. And he spoke of her fondly.

Dirt flew off Tinker's hooves in waves of dust. Becca covered her mouth with a hankie and continued toward the Cain Ranch. The sky had turned from bright blue and now included some deep crimson creeping out west of her. Her gaze lingered on the beautiful sight longer than she'd intended. Before she knew it, she'd ridden to the edge of Blanche's land.

Tinker slowed and they rode close to the house. As Becca passed the well in front, her eyes came to rest on a horse, tied casually to the hitch in the front.

Charger?

Well, of course, he'd probably come to ask if she knew of anyone to help with the fences. Perhaps inquire if she knew of interested hired hands. And perhaps not. Hadn't he recently told her he didn't need Jeremy much longer now that the apples were nearly done?

Becca stopped. Put a hand on her heart. Then why was he here? What could he possibly want with Blanche Cain?

Maybe Jared hadn't come to see about hired help at all, but to see Blanche. After all, they had spent half a night together after his fall. Becca had no way of knowing what they meant to each other. He had said they'd known each other for a long time. Were friends. All that mattered at the moment was that Jared was here and Becca was intruding.

She pulled on the reins. Tinker fought against her

touch and jerked toward Charger. Becca tugged, but the fool horse acted more like a mule than a mare. She couldn't be caught here, practically staring in Blanche's windows. She jumped down, hauled once more on Tinker's rein and then turned toward the path. Alone.

Well, fine, then. She would walk home.

## Chapter 13

Jared thanked Blanche with a hug and a peck on her cheek. Her smile followed him all the way to Charger's side. He'd been right to come here. After all, a man had to do certain things. And he needed to know he had someone to count on. Blanche had been the solution to his problem. "I owe you."

"You do. Your visiting now and then will be payment enough. I've missed having you around, especially since—"

"Don't give it a thought. I'm grateful to you."

But as he cautiously threw his leg over the saddle, Charger's ears pricked up. Jared turned. Tinker? A few feet from the well, his mare, saddled and obviously having been ridden, waited patiently to go home.

"How'd you get here, girl? Becca bring you? Where is she?" He cupped his hands to his mouth. "Becca?"

Blanche dashed from the porch. "Jared? What's all the fuss about?" She lifted her skirts and ran toward him. "Is Becca here? Where did Tinker come from?"

"I don't know. Would you go check in the barn? If she's not here, Tinker could have thrown her." Remembering being tossed, he felt his chest heaving. "Hurry, Blanche."

He rode a ways along the path while Blanche searched the outbuildings. No Becca. Dizzy from the pain in his leg, Jared turned back to Blanche's.

Sweat dripping around her hair, Blanche ran to meet him.

"Any sign of her?"

"No, Jared. I'm sorry. She's not here. Is it possible Tinker simply ran off?"

He slid from the saddle and examined the mare. "No, see here? She was bringing something to your house." He groaned. "Some of the dessert she made today. Blanche, Becca was here. This is no runaway horse. She must have come here and then thought…"

"Surely not. Oh, Jared, you have to find her and set her straight. She must be so upset."

"Stable Tinker for me, will you?"

Jared threw away all caution and rode Charger harder than he ever had before. With his leg stuffed into the stirrup, he winced with each shift of Charger's body, but he didn't care. He must find her.

Tears blinding her eyes, Becca did her best to stay on the path as she ran. Her only choice in this whole mess was to retrieve her one outfit from the ranch and escape to town. There, she would find a job until she could get a ticket to home…to somewhere. Perhaps if she rode the train to Chicago, she would remember. Who she was, where she'd come from. Maybe…

After packing the small satchel, the walk toward town eventually cleared her head. With the sun setting behind her, shadows danced over the ground and soon enough, she feared walking around the grove of trees near Lone Rock. The gnarled branches resembled monsters. She stopped in one place and sat against a rock. The ranch had grown smaller in the distance. So small that in the dusk, she could barely make out the shape of the barn anymore. She leaned back and closed her eyes. Jared and that Cain woman must have been involved before she arrived. Then why did he want a mail-order bride in the first place? Bringing a woman all the way out here just to push her aside seemed cruel, too cruel for Jared. He had shown her nothing but kindness, until now. A tear trickled from her eye and she swiped at it before the drop could splatter on her clothes. She wasn't about to waste one more tear on Jared Callahan.

She would have to beg for a job in town. Before talking to anyone else, she would go see Dr. Parker. He might know of a possible position.

A noise startled her. Lifting her head, she opened her eyes. In the shadows, a silhouette. Two bright eyes and a low growl.

Tumbling head over petticoats, Becca fell at least thirty feet before her skirt caught on a branch. It snapped, but she landed with a thud on a craggy narrow ledge of rock. She dug her fingers into the stump of growth still attached to the overhanging edge but it came off into her hands. Her heart pounded so hard she thought her ribs might break through her chest.

*Calm down. Don't panic yet. Jared said he came this*

*way with a mule before. If I just stay still, someone will find me.* But who? No one even knew she was missing and coyotes didn't tell tales.

Just then, she heard another cry from above. Was the animal still there? Would it find its way over the edge? She shivered, drawing her arms around her chest. Jared had told her coyotes didn't bother humans. But wolves did.

Jared shouted at the front door. "Becca! Where are you? Are you here?" He pushed his way into the house, checking each room. Then he grabbed the cane tighter and stumbled as quickly for the barn as possible, limping badly now. "Becca? Where are you? I found Tinker. What happened to you?"

Where could she have gone? Why was she at Blanche's in the first place? He heaved himself onto Charger's back for the third time that day. His leg barely tucked into the stirrup this time. Not much strength was left in his muscles and the throbbing was unbearable. But there was no time to lose; he had to find her before dark settled in. Being lost in the darkness didn't bode well for anyone, let alone a young woman still learning the lay of the land.

All along the path back to Blanche's, he continued calling her name. He looked behind trees, stopped Charger periodically and called her name over every inch of ground between the two properties.

Arriving at Blanche's again, he limped to the house. He practically tugged Blanche's arm from the socket. "Have you seen her? Did she come back here?"

"Jared, hold your horses. No, she's not here. I don't need to ask if you were successful."

"She's not home. Nowhere this side of my property. There would be no reason for her to go east. Not on foot, not alone."

Blanche's face darkened. "You two have a spat?"

"What? No." Not a spat. Not really. But he had been plenty angry when she'd stepped away from him. Like always, just the hired hand and the boss. Surely that wouldn't have been enough for her to run away. Of course, she might have assumed he planned to be forward, forget his promise. How could she? A promise was just that and he'd never gone back on one in his life. No, there had to be another reason for such irrational behavior.

"I'm thinking you aren't telling me the whole story, Jared Callahan. I know it's not likely, but did you hurt that girl?"

"No! Of course not. And I'm not going to stand here flapping my jaw when she's out there all by herself. Now, if you'd be kind enough to be on the lookout. If she should show up here, please hitch the wagon and see her home. I'll keep checkin' at the house for the two of you. In the meantime, I plan to cover every inch of this land until I find her. If I don't find her here I'll head to town."

"Get some water to take with you." He shook his head, but Blanche insisted, and after a heated exchange, he finally filled a canteen at the well before riding off.

Now the sun was down, and cool air settled like a layer of frost against her skin. Before morning, she would be even colder. Coyotes didn't sound like her worst enemy at the moment.

*Lord, I've tried to be honest and true to Jared since I*

*came. I'm so sorry I didn't tell him about the letters and
my signature. I simply didn't know what to do. Please,
Lord, show Jared where I am. Help me.*

A small movement rippled under her skirt. Becca
panicked and shoved away from the skittering motion.
Her palm slid over the edge and she screamed. She
jerked back, her breath coming in sharp gasps. She had
nearly gone over the side. But that tingling sensation…
She lifted the edge of her skirt. A daddy longlegs
crawled out from under, faster than she'd ever seen one
move. She must have scared him more than he did her.

Becca gave a nervous laugh and scooted her back
against the stone. The branch made a good place to put
her feet up, to rest them. Anything to feel a bit normal.
She pretended she sat in the front room of the house.
She faced the fireplace, her feet resting on an ottoman.
Jared sat in the big wing chair, cleaning his rifle.

*He turned, smiled her direction. "Are you thirsty? I
thought about getting a cup of coffee."*

Then the daydream took on a life of its own as she
tried to will herself anywhere but here.

*"I might get another piece of that apple pie. Where
did you learn to cook like that, Becca?"*

*She blinked. "I don't remember."*

*He stopped behind her chair, caressed her chin with
his thumb. "It doesn't matter. I'd love you if you couldn't
cook at all." His eyes reflected the firelight. More important, they reflected the warmth of his love.*

Becca shivered and rubbed her arms. Dark settled
over the valley in deep purples and grays. Shadowy fig-
ures scurried below. Wolves? Coyotes? Snakes!

*"And I love you, Jared." Her arms encircled his
neck. She didn't worry about back home. She only cared*

*about Jared. In that moment, his head dipped to meet hers and his lips covered her mouth. Inviting and sure, he sought to show her all the love that was in him, and she responded to his kiss.*

Her eyes shot open. Just a daydream. There was no Jared holding her. No kiss to warm her heart. Only a dangerous edge over which she might fall any minute if she didn't take care. And yet the dream had seemed so real that she closed her eyes to the potential danger. If she kept thinking of Jared, she might be able to keep the cold away.

*They were in front of the fireplace again. And she succumbed to the heat of the crackling logs.*

*"You were brought here for a reason, Becca. Thank you for telling me about the letters. But why did you wait so long?"*

*"I was afraid you'd send me away."* And he would have, wouldn't he?

*"Never. I loved you from the second you stepped out of the wagon. I just knew you were the love I'd been waiting for."*

*She bit the side of her cheek, pondering whether or not he was simply being kind, as he usually was.*

*"And I, you."*

*"You could have fooled me, Becca."*

*"I didn't want to appear forward."*

*He walked around her chair, took her face in his hands. When she didn't pull away, he leaned closer until he touched the end of her nose with his. Then the smile she had grown to love filled her heart. "You certainly were not that. I had to fight for you, my love."*

*Then he wrapped an arm around her shoulders and drew her against him. "But you were worth the fight."*

*He covered her mouth with his lips, softly at first, but then he lifted her into his arms and nuzzled her neck. "Let's forget about the rest of the world. Tonight, you are my sweet, sweet Becca."*

"Becca! Do you hear me? Where are you?" Jared struggled to stay erect in the saddle. His leg twitched and beat a steady rhythm of pain. His head pounded from all the yelling. No one in town had seen her; he had even gone so far as to enter the Last Chance Saloon and talk with Fletcher, but the weasel assured him he hadn't seen her.

Doc Parker hemmed and hawed, but in the end, he didn't have a clue, either. Where could she have gone?

He drew nearer the edge of Lone Rock and listened. Coyotes scurried in the distance. There must be a lost calf or lamb. Coyotes flocked to any small animal, but never seemed to bother humans. Cupping his hand to his ear, he strained to hear, but all he heard were yips and barks.

A glance at his pant leg showed him he had done too much. Blood oozed from just above his boot and soaked through the material of his jeans. He winced as he touched the leg and drew back red fingers. If he didn't dress the wound, he would pass out and then he wouldn't be in any condition to look for her.

Jared returned to his ranch, where he fed Charger and then headed straight for the kitchen to redress his injured leg. He slipped off his boots and dropped his pants. The wound had grown to an angry red. Painful to the touch, he washed away the blood and wrapped his leg with clean cloths.

His head swirled. Dizzy, light-headed. He had to get

off the leg for a few minutes before he passed out from the pain. Grabbing a piece of bread from a drawer, he carried it to the bedroom, something he never did. But tonight was an exception. Tonight he had to try and gain some strength before going back out to search for Becca.

Stretched out on the bed, he felt sweat trickling over his forehead into his eyes. Sweat? He hadn't started a fire; how could he be sweating? He turned on his side to take the pressure off his leg for just a few minutes.

## Chapter 14

Becca awoke to the screech of a hawk overhead. Her breath caught in fascination as she watched it swoop down and pluck a mouse from the ledge a few feet away. She dug her numb and tingly toes against the stone and pushed with all her might. The bird didn't give her a single glance; it had what it wanted—a meal. Then she saw past the scene to the wall of rock beyond her, filled with one outcropping of cold stone after another. Almost like giant steps leading to the valley below; perhaps that was how the mules made their way down the side of the cliff.

Her fingers reached for her head. Pain swelled under her hand, like after the train accident. Nothing she could do about it right now. She had to figure out a way to crawl up or down. Numb as she was, Becca knew she wouldn't last another night of low temperatures. Jared had been right; the cold settled in early in Minnesota.

So thirsty. Her eyes fluttered shut to stop the pitch of pain and from dwelling on what had happened to her—last night? Had she been here but one night? Even with the sun coming up, the cold didn't go away. Her insides shivered with icy fingers tapping along her spine and over her shoulders. She pulled a hand to her cheek; her fingertips, like ice, sent another chill through her. She shrugged against the massive stone once more. Maybe the sun would take away the chill. Or maybe not.

One thing played out in her mind with certainty. If she didn't get off this ledge, she would die. A yipping bark below her caught her attention. Yes, she would die, either from the elements or some wild animal.

When she opened her mouth to scream for help, a voice in her aching head quieted her. What if those animals were still at the top of the cliff? What if Jared had come to find her but a coyote or wolf had harmed him? *Oh, Lord. Please protect Jared. This is all my fault.*

Her lips drooped again, so tired was she from the chilling night. And now all she could do was sit here and wait for help to come, or wait to… She wouldn't allow herself to think that.

The next thing Jared knew, a shaft of light eased his eyes open. He jumped from bed and nearly collapsed on his bad leg. Massaging around the throbbing wound until he had feeling again, he allowed his fingers to bring the flesh to life once more. He'd fallen asleep when he should have been out looking for Becca. With a fear and dread born of his love for her, he wobbled to the kitchen. He splashed cold water on his face from the pitcher in the corner. Then he poured yesterday's coffee into a cup and drank it, stale and bitter. Grabbing the remaining slice of bread, he stumbled to the barn, dragging his sore leg like a bird's broken wing. Jared knew if he ever wanted to find Becca alive, he had to go now, pain or no pain. He'd wasted enough time.

He stumbled to the barn, his leg a reminder he wasn't out of the woods yet.

Charger didn't balk at all having the saddle thrown onto him. Jared pulled the cinch tight and tossed himself immediately onto the stallion's back. He heard the cows' pitiful cries and opened the small gate that separated them from the calves, but he didn't stop long enough to offer relief. Becca could be crying, as well.

He looped his canteen over the saddle horn and rode away from the barn, unsure where to go first. If not in town, where could she have gone? There weren't many places to hide around his ranch, and he had checked everywhere. She was not in town, not at the ranch, not on the road to town or the road to Blanche's. What was left?

He choked down dread. Time to head back to Lone Rock.

The sun deceived Becca. Through hopeful eyes, the rays looked warm and inviting, but they only served to make her miss home, where the fireplace no doubt burned hot and strong.

Her own fingers reached toward the imaginary fire, but cold cinders met them, so she snatched them back. She licked her lips to wet them; dry, flaky skin came off on her tongue. She spit over the edge and felt warmth at last as a tear trickled down her face.

If only she hadn't run away. She would be warm all over. And comfortable. She and Jared might be sitting at the table sharing a meal—more of the brown Betty with sweet caramel sauce. She shook her hair from her eyes. Her foolishness had caused this situation. Bad choices that confronted her...here...on the edge of Lone Rock.

An unexpected giggle escaped her lips. Brown Betty. How droll that she should think about that now. Chattering teeth followed the laughter and she hesitated a second, wondering who they belonged to. Sleep crept over her and the cold slipped further away. Increasing warmth encircled her body like a shining rainbow. The sun must be nearly overhead now for that kind of heat. A huge sigh ripped from her chest. She felt peace at last.

At the last minute, Jared whirled Charger around and headed toward town. If Becca wasn't at the ranch and not at Blanche's, she had to be in town. He would inspect every building from the inside out by gunpoint if he had to. He *would* find Becca.

And no one had better attempt to stop him.

Arriving at the general store, he questioned not only the owner, but the customers. No one had seen her.

Mrs. Merriwether, known to be a mean and nasty gossip, pointed across the street. "You might want to check the saloon. I heard tell they have a new girl there. After all, what can you expect from a stranger coming in on the train and no one to meet her? Mail-order bride, indeed! You mark my words, young Mr. Callahan—"

"Stop!" Jared's teeth ground. If only she were a man. "I met her, Mrs. Merriwether. I met her at the train, and I intend to find out who wants to hurt her. Perhaps gossipy old hens with nothing better to do with their time than slander young women. Honorable young women, by the way. My wife!"

Her eyes teared. When she walked away, the starch

had left her bloomers. Good. Because if she had stayed… Guilt swirled over him. He should apologize, but not now.

One business after another without results. No one had seen Becca and no one had heard a word about her…until he entered the Last Chance. He questioned the bartender, Johnny, but he had nothing to say. Johnny deferred to Fletcher, who leaned against the piano in the corner plunking on keys, creating a hideous noise. Everyone waited to see what he would do.

Jared stared into the eyes of a monster when he confronted Fletcher. "Tell me what you know."

Fletcher chuckled and resumed plunking on the keys. "What makes you think I know anything about your wife? I have my hands full here." He indicated the girls standing near the bar. "You think I have time to keep track of your problems, too? I can assure you, these ladies keep me busy enough."

With that, Fletcher got up and left the room.

Jared walked toward the girl he'd seen fly through the saloon window. "Can we talk…"

"Jesse. My name's Jesse."

"Well, then, Jesse. I have a couple questions."

Jesse cleared her throat when Jared pulled her aside. "I don't know nothing about your wife, Mr. Callahan. I wish I did." But her eyes said otherwise.

"Jesse, I heard what happened to you. And I'm sorry, but if I don't find Becca, I'm afraid she's going to die. Do you want that on your conscience?"

"My conscience? I didn't do nothing. I only saw when—"

"When what?"

"Well, Mr. Fletcher brought back a bag with him. Only, it was a lady's bag, nothing a man would carry."

No longer able to distinguish between reality and fantasy, Becca wished for death to come. It had to be better than this. She pulled her tongue over her lips again, this time feeling nothing but an old dry chunk of leather. Water...

If she were home with her family, she wouldn't be going through this...her family? She had a family. Her lids opened, forcing her to take in her surroundings yet again. She had a family. She pictured a mother, a father, a very handsome young man and a small girl, no older than two or three.

She held the youngster's hand, the young man held the girl's other hand and they swung her between them. He smiled at her; she smiled back. A dry cough choked her as she dwelled on the images in her head. She could see them as clearly as if they stood before her. And she knew them. Knew them well.

Oh, she was married and with a daughter. A huge gasp escaped her lips as she fell back. *Lord, this can't be. Please take me home to be with You. I can't face what I've done here. If there's family waiting for me, I don't know who and I don't know where. If You are truly there, as Jared says, take me home. I'm not afraid to die, only to live and find out what trouble I have caused for Jared as well as my family.*

As she allowed her body to succumb to the inevitability of dying, familiar sounds enclosed her. Try as she might, she wasn't able to respond.

"Becca! Becca, are you down there?"

His deep, comforting voice filled the air. A horse's

snort, a bird's squawk, the coyote again. That little girl laughing at her side.

"Becca!"

The sweet song of her name wrapped her in peace, and at last, she was able to understand all she'd been searching for. She had to be honest: whether or not she had a husband somewhere, she had fallen helplessly in love with Jared Callahan. If she ever, by some miracle, crawled out of here, he couldn't know. He was a good man, too kind to be involved in a scandal of this magnitude. But before she could leave and try to make amends, she had to see his handsome face one last time.

"Becca, are you there?"

Pushing away from the wall, she opened her mouth to speak, but her dry, sandy throat only whispered his name.

Jared strained to see over the edge; he couldn't lean far enough to tell whether or not there was movement on that ledge below. Maybe it was only an animal or shadows, but he had to be sure. There was only one way to do that; he would have to lower himself over the edge. Even a mule wouldn't be able to approach from this side of the cliff.

He threw his leg over Charger and bolted for Blanche's. He was going to need help.

What should have been a short trip became a lengthy ride of torment. His Becca might be hanging on to the edge of Lone Rock, ready to fall. Had he heard a cry before he left? If only he'd taken her in his arms and told her he loved her in the weeks they'd been married. He'd had so many opportunities, but instead of comforting her, caring for her, he had waited. Waited for her to let him know how she felt. Pride! And now he was left with *if only.*

He kicked into Charger's side. "Let's go, boy."

With Blanche barreling behind him in the wagon, Jared wasted no time returning to Lone Rock. With heavy lengths of rope, a full canteen, two blankets and Charger leading, they headed back toward Lone Rock. Jared had prepared the best he could in order to slide himself over the side of the cliff. It would be her only chance.

As he approached the edge, he pulled Charger away from the side and directed Blanche to pull the wagon near the cliff. Then she set the brake and he tied two ropes to the corner of the wagon bed, checking to be sure they were tight enough to support him and, hopefully, her.

"Keep a watch on the ropes. I don't want to keep falling. And remember, once I'm down, if I have her, I'll tug on this second rope here. You'll have about five minutes to loop it over the saddle horn so Charger can pull us up. Don't forget. I haven't the strength to get us both up."

"Don't you worry about that. You just get down there. I'm praying, Jared. Praying hard."

Then he looped the end of second rope over his shoulder. He eased himself down with the help of the first.

"Don't let it go now," he shouted to the top. If Becca were over the edge, he had to find her, get her home and warmed up right away. Last night had been dreadfully cold.

With two tight knots, he'd circled himself into the rope and lowered himself over the edge carefully, but still, pain ricocheted through his calf, forcing him to rely on his good leg alone. Hand over hand, he headed backward and down, all the while calling Becca's name. The rope burned as the scratchy fibers slid through his fingers. In no time at all he had bloody scratches from his fingertips to his wrists. But he couldn't dwell on that right now. Only Becca mattered.

Halfway down, he was able to see over the outcropping of rock. Not an animal, but his wife. "She's here, Blanche. I see her."

He didn't wait for a response but turned his attention to his wife. "I'm coming. Don't worry, Becca, I'm here. Just stay back from that ledge."

As he said the words, his hand slipped and he fell a good ten feet, enough to get his heart pumping like a fire engine. He grasped the side of Lone Rock's face with one hand and the rope with the other, snatching for any sharp rock to lend extra support. Blood covered the rock's face as his grip tightened. Over his shoulder, he shouted Becca's name over and over. At last, a faint sound reached his ear. The sweet, blessed sound of her voice.

"Here…down…here." Faint, but most assuredly Becca. At least he knew she was alive.

No sooner had she cried out than Jared threw caution out and increased his descent. His leg slammed the side of the rocky drop; he winced. How could he help Becca when he could barely help himself? Blood, this time flowing heavily, stained his pant leg.

Patience. He had to be patient. Hand over hand. One

foot at a time. He wasn't doing this to become her hero. He was a man in love, out to save his wife.

Her cries, pitiful and growing weaker, burrowed into his heart. "I'm coming. Almost there."

# Chapter 15

"Jared?" Her face lit like Fourth of July fireworks. "Jared!" She seemed barely to be holding on, and he circled her with his arms. "You found me."

"There, now. You'll be all right."

"Jared, is it really you? I thought for a minute—"

He put a finger to her lips. "It's okay, Becca. Shhh, everything's going to be all right." Maybe now, maybe here they would find the trust they sorely needed. He shook his head; no time for that now. If only he could get her off the face of the cliff. He pulled the top from the canteen. Badly dehydrated, she needed that addressed first. "Here, take a drink."

Water dribbled from her dry lips. "I thought...I thought I'd never see you again."

"What happened?"

"An animal near the edge and I...I guess I jumped over to get out of its way. I heard it howling all night."

His temple flared with a pounding pain all the way to the back of his head. He should have been there for her. "We'll talk back at the house. You've had enough excitement for one day. Let's get you secured into this other rope. And don't worry. I'll hold on to you as we're pulled up."

He gave a tug on the second rope and then snatched the length from his shoulder to make a harness for Becca. He kept the first rope snug around him. They could both go up with Charger helping. She wrapped her arms around him. Still, her deadweight would be difficult as Jared had to secure her and lift hand over hand. His arms tightened into steel knots as he grasped the rope and pulled.

He'd never thought about it much, but he was mighty happy for his powerful upper body. He waited for the rope to tighten around Becca and then he began to haul them up.

Becca buried her head against his back, her arms like ropes of their own connecting her body to his. Tears soaked his shirt. How could she tell him her tears were from the memories she had begun to have? Here he was, her hero, and when they returned to the ranch, her responsibility would be to tell him the truth, a truth that would tear them apart. She looked up; the light blinded her.

"Becca, keep your head down. Tight against me. If you lean back, we'll both go over the side.

"S-sorry." She tried to be still, but everything in her cried out to be free of the cliff.

"Don't be sorry, just be safe." His muscles strained

under his shirt as he guided their ascent. "I don't know what I would have done if I'd lost you."

If he could look into her eyes, would he kiss her? She couldn't allow it. Not with the possibility of a husband and child at home. So she clasped him closer and hid her face in the rough fabric of his shirt. Her voice cracked when she cried, "Don't let go of me."

Jared's sigh echoed over the valley and came to rest in her ears.

"Never."

Everything in Jared wanted to stop, wrap Becca in his arms and kiss her. He hadn't done one thing right since he'd welcomed her off the wagon the day of the derailment. And here he was, still stumbling over words, ideas, intentions. Was he a man or a pathetic hound dog? He loved her. That's right—loved. The sooner he faced facts, the sooner he would be able to hold her, calm her, love her as his wife. His wife!

The absurdity of wanting to stop now sent a shudder through him. For the moment, all he should keep thinking about was putting one hand over the other until Charger pulled them to the top. The next few feet would be the most crucial.

"Becca, we're going over the outcropping. Hold tight."

She dug her hands into his chest. "All right."

He pulled in a deep breath, but as she squeezed his chest, his ribs rebelled. Pain shot across his chest until the air whooshed out. *Don't panic. You can do this.* "Stay close, Becca."

"Now!" Keeping his gaze on the edge of the cliff, he

guided them over the rocky structure and tugged hard on the ropes. His legs, throbbing from pain and exertion, pushed hard against the stone. It was getting more difficult to breathe, his heart like a pounding hammer in his chest. If he stopped now because of the pain, they would both die as Charger pulled, smashing them against the rock.

Becca closed her eyes and allowed the fluffy softness of the quilt to enclose her. Everything in her told her to rise and tend to Jared's leg, but she didn't seem to be able to warm up after her night on the cliff.

Jared offered her more broth. "Becca. We have to talk."

Her eyes couldn't meet his. "I know."

"We've not really talked since you arrived on the train." His fingers curled around hers and ripples of contentment soared through her. "If we want to have a marriage, we need to be able to trust each other. Why did you leave Tinker and run home?"

"So much to tell you." But not now. She couldn't bring up Blanche when she had secrets of her own. Jealous? She had no right. Somewhere out there was a family waiting for her to return to them. How could she be here in Jared's home telling him she was jealous of Blanche Cain? Especially after she'd helped save Becca's life?

He stroked her forehead and she pressed into his touch. No! She had to think of her other family. She turned her head aside.

"Becca, I might understand. Do you think…I mean, did you think I was seeing Blanche? Is that it?"

Her eyes fluttered open and she nodded in spite of her best efforts to draw a line between them.

"Listen up." Jared leaned in, cupped her chin with his hand. "I went to purchase a filly for you. Blanche has the sweetest little palomino and I thought you could use her to ride. For us. So we could ride together in the mornings."

"You have so many horses already."

"But none that would be a right fit for you. I wanted a horse for your own, Becca. You already share all of these with me. I wanted a filly that would truly be yours. Just yours to ride and take care of."

"Oh, Jared." She should have known. No matter that she made a mess of things, he was making plans for them. For her comfort. Always thinking of her before himself.

"It's okay."

"No, it's not. What I thought! And I had no right. No right at all."

He smoothed the hair from her eyes. "Shhh. We'll talk about all this later. Once you're feeling better."

She pulled the quilt around her shoulders and flipped over to face the wall. Humiliation settled in and consumed her with tears.

Jared struggled to reach the kitchen with the cup in his hands. He slumped into a chair and dropped his head onto his forearm. Sleep. If only he could get some sleep while Becca did the same, but Blanche was doing all his work in the barn and he felt funny about that. This marriage hadn't turned out at all as he had planned. The wound on his leg had reopened and he was barely able to walk. His wife slept in her own room, not knowing who she was. And his ranch was worse off than it had been just two months ago. Where had their plans gone? Why hadn't God allowed this relationship to grow? Was he being punished for advertising for a bride instead of waiting on God?

He couldn't blame God. Actually, he had no one to blame but himself.

Standing shot hot flashes of pain through his leg and his chest. But he needed to get back to work. The sweet smell of hay and manure pulled him into the horses' stalls. "There you go, fella." Charger swished his tail, no longer frightened by the craziness of the past few days. Jared reached into his pocket. "Here. Have an apple for all your efforts." He brushed the horse's sides until the animal shone. "You deserve better, boy. Let's give you a rest for a while. How's that sound? Maybe find you a pretty little filly who has Charger on her mind?" Or a pretty little filly named Becca with Jared on her mind.

"You talkin' to yourself, Jared?"

"Sorry, almost forgot you were here, Blanche. Why don't you go on now? I've got Becca settled in the house and you've taken care of the animals. I don't know how I'll ever thank you."

"When you pay for that filly, I'll add a small tip to her fee." A grin covered her face and Jared knew at that moment, Blanche would always be one of his best friends, and now one of Becca's.

He should really go for Doc, just to be sure Becca was all right.

"On second thought, could you stay a bit longer?"

Blanche lifted one of the pails of milk and cocked her head. "Of course, why?"

"I'm going to ride into town for Dr. Parker. Let him have a look at Becca and maybe dress this leg again."

"Mighty long way to go just to see Doc."

"I have other business, if you must know."

"You'll be all right riding like that?"

"If you're here, I won't worry. And yes, I'll be fine."

"Take care of yourself, Jared."

What he really planned to do was find out why Jesse thought Fletcher might have information about Becca. After cleaning and bandaging his leg and checking one more time on Becca, Jared saddled his horse. Each shift of his weight in the saddle drew a new round of sweat to his brow. And the trip into town this time around seemed to take forever.

When he arrived in front of the saloon, he sat for a bit, deciding how to approach the man inside. He eased off Charger and looped the reins over the hitching post. *Don't forget, you're a praying man. Don't make a fool of yourself. Help me to do the right thing, Lord.* Time for some real answers to his questions. He limped forward and entered the saloon, straightening at the last minute, trying his best to hide his injuries.

He found Fletcher behind the bar. "What did you do with Becca's bag?"

Fletcher eyed him warily. Then his gaze fell on Jesse as she dashed from the room. "I don't know what you're talking about."

"Jesse told me you took her satchel at the train wreck. That you've been bragging about it. Becca has a right to—"

"She's not Rebecca Layne, you idiot! She's not who you think at all!"

Too tired to care whether or not Fletcher got the upper hand, Jared slumped into the nearest chair. "What do you mean? How do you know that?" Jared knew she wasn't Rebecca Layne, but how could Fletcher, and how would that affect Becca?

"I found her satchel when I was out riding last week. Haven't had a chance to take it to her. I never brought it from the train wreck. Jesse's talking nonsense."

"But she said…"

Jesse dashed back into the room, a small reticule in her hands. "Here." She pointed at Fletcher, now standing, brushing at his clothes. "He won't tell you, but I will."

"Shut up, you fool!" He turned to Jared. "She's rambling, drunk. Doesn't know what she's saying."

"I am not drunk! I don't know much, Mr. Fletcher, but I know this. You can't keep no more secrets about Mrs. Callahan. I don't care none what happens to me, but she's a good soul. And you stole from her. You known all along where she come from and all."

Fletcher inched a step toward the saloon girl, fists raised, but Jared jumped between them. He used his body to protect her, sad protection that it provided. "Jesse, I'll buy you a train ticket anywhere you want to go. Will you accompany me to the sheriff and tell him all you know about Becca?"

"I will, sir." She glared at Fletcher. "And I'll be tellin' him the whole truth about Mr. Fletcher here."

"You'll shut your mouth, Jesse."

"Not no longer I won't." The girl drew back, shook

when she spoke, but Jared didn't miss the note of defiance in her tone.

He reached for his holster and pulled out his revolver. "Let's go, Fletcher. I'm as anxious to hear what Jesse has to say, and I'm sure Sheriff Morgan will be, too."

# Chapter 16

"I swear I didn't know nothin' till I found him in the back room this morning. Mr. Fletcher there was goin' through the bag. He was some mad when he saw me standing in the doorway. I swear, Sheriff Morgan. I didn't know nothin' till then."

Fletcher aimed a narrowed gaze at Jesse. "You fool. You've spoiled everything." His head, having lost its arrogant stature, dipped against his chest. "Who would have thought a nothing like you could ruin my plans?"

The sheriff hit the edge of the chair where Fletcher sat. "What might those plans be, Mr. Fletcher?"

"I'll talk to you once Mr. Callahan removes himself from your office."

Jared winced. While he longed to have the entire story spelled out, he also longed to be with Becca. Explain the letter from Miss Layne. "May I have her bag, Sheriff?"

"Sure enough. I don't s'pose there's any reason to keep it. I have an inventory of everything that's left." He looked at Fletcher. "What'd you do with the jewelry and money?"

Jesse grabbed the sheriff's shirtsleeve. "Probably gambled away the money, but the jewelry's in the saloon's safe. I saw him put it there. Pretty it was. And he let me touch one of the pieces."

Fletcher's eyes twitched. "Shut up, you worthless girl."

She shivered, her arms hugging her chest. "Then he slapped me and told me I was no good. Shouldn't be touching the lady's things."

The sheriff leaned against his desk, his arms resting on an ample belly. He stared at Fletcher. "I've had my eyes on you. When you bought the saloon, I had a bad feeling you were up to no good. Just a nice town watering hole, I think you said. Wanted to spiff it up a bit. Make the town proud."

Fletcher smirked in a way that made Jared want to slug him, but he held back, allowed the sheriff to do his job.

The sheriff leaned in, close enough to feel the scoundrel's breath on his face. "And how did you come to know Mrs. Callahan?"

"I might say, and I might not."

Jared balled his fist again and pressed it under Fletcher's nose.

"All right, all right. I heard her telling a lady on the train she was heading out West to set up a mercantile somewhere in South Dakota. Wanted a chance to start over, whatever that meant. When the lady asked her about how she planned to do it, she said she had some jewelry and money set aside. All these grand plans. For a woman. Not likely."

His heart in his throat, Jared pressed forward. "And what else did she tell her?"

"Just that she had enough to start up the business. I'll repay everything." He glanced at the sheriff. "No reason to hold me. I haven't done a thing wrong other than pick up a lady's bag that I found."

Jesse's face burned red. "That's not true, Fletcher. You told me you took it from the train wreck."

Jared slammed a fist into his palm. "Sheriff, unless you want me finding out the truth from this man the hard way, I suggest—"

The sheriff held up his hand, his gaze not wavering from Fletcher. "He'll tell us. Tell us all we want to know. Won't you, mister?"

His smirk had long since left his face. He even kept his gaze from Jesse when he said, "I've told you all I know. I'll give all her whatnots back. Then leave town."

The sheriff nodded. "You'll leave for good? What about your girls?"

Fletcher rose, but Jared didn't leave his side. "Yes. I'll go. I don't care a bit what those girls do. No loyalty, no loss."

Jesse cringed against the wall.

"But first, you're going tell Mr. Callahan here all there is to tell. And if I find out you're lying about any of it, I'll lock you up so fast—"

Fletcher raised his hand. "No need to get riled. If you gentlemen will take a seat and stop pacing, I'll tell you everything from the beginning. All nice and legal-like. I have done absolutely nothing wrong."

Jesse's lip trembled. "What's gonna happen to me? And the other girls if he up and goes?"

The sheriff hooked a thumb in the direction of Cain's ranch and said to Jared, "Blanche's pa used to run the saloon. I figure I'm going to put Jesse out at her place. She always said if any of the girls needed a place to stay, they could stay with her. I'll be taking her up on it."

"No one will bother them?" Jared asked.

"I feel sorry for anyone who tries to get the best of Blanche Cain. She's the best shot around. Don't let her looks fool anyone."

Jared chuckled at last, knowing the sheriff spoke the truth. "All right, Mr. Fletcher. Why not tell us all you know?"

Becca rested her head against the back of the swing. The motion lulled her. The time had come when she had to explain to Jared what she remembered. Would he give her the money to return on the train? Return where? Though memories were starting, she still didn't know exactly where she'd come from.

But the little girl. She had an image of that child in a frilly dress.

Frilly dress? She sat straighter. *That's it.* She sewed dresses for the youngster. She was sure of it. Beautiful frocks with matching bonnets. Long golden ringlets danced around the tie under the girl's chin. Of course. She closed her eyes and felt the silky fabric sifting through her fingers. Her little girl? She must be. The child was the image of what Becca must have looked like at that age. All blond ringlets and blue eyes.

*Oh, Jared. I'm so sorry I put you through this marriage. Thank heavens you were a patient man willing to wait...* Her teeth chattered. *What if...* Thankfully what if had never happened.

Her feet tapped a determined rhythm as she reentered the house. She had to put together the few things that belonged to her. When he came home, they would eat dinner and have that long-awaited talk. Then she could find work in town until she had enough money to go home.

She sniffed the air. The beans bubbled on the back of the stove. A cup of coffee would taste fine, but exhaustion from her memories had taken priority. She walked over and moved the kettle toward the front so it wouldn't burn. After tending the fire, she strolled to her room, took off her shoes and climbed under the warm, comforting quilt.

"Becca!"

She sat up and rubbed her eyes. Lands, she'd fallen asleep when packing should have been her priority.

Listening to Jared's boots on the porch, she sighed. The limp was so pronounced. He must be in a great deal of pain. And yet what she had to tell him would cause him even more pain. All because the train didn't stay on the tracks. Like her life since the accident. She hadn't been able to stay on track. Now they both had to face the reality of her memories. She was married, had a husband and a precious little girl. While the memory had returned, she found it strange she didn't feel a connection to them other than the knowledge that she had sewn the dress.

She slid her legs over the edge of the bed and smoothed her hair. Struggling with her shoes, she sucked back a breath as Jared strode around the corner.

"Dinner's almost ready."

"You fixed dinner?"

"Blanche put some beans on and baked bread. I told her to go on home. I'd be fine." She wiped hair from her eyes. "She's a good friend, Jared. I'm sorry about what I thought."

His voice was soft and gentle, as if he were talking to a child. "And I'm as hungry as a bear, but that's not all I care about. And yes, Blanche is a wonderful friend…to both of us."

"Your leg?" Her gaze stayed locked on the floor. She was too embarrassed to look him in the eye, ashamed of the mess she'd gotten both of them into. And here he was, in pain from pulling her off the face of the cliff.

"No, Caroline. Not my leg, either."

Caroline? She looked up. He held a good-size satchel in his hands. Where had that come from? *Caroline?*

Suddenly her head spun as she reached out for the bed. Calming, blissful darkness enveloped her.

Her brow felt soft as he brushed it with the cool cloth. Maybe it hadn't been such a wise idea to call her by her given name. Must have been a shock. He took in the pale cheeks, the long lashes and the curls plastered to her forehead. Any minute now, Caroline would wake up, and hopefully she would remember her name and where she came from, and they could start over.

Lifting her head, he offered a drink of the strong coffee that had been warming since morning. "Becca?"

Her lips touched the edge of the cup as those eyes, oh, those beautiful eyes, opened. "Thank you. What did you call me before? And why?"

He gently let go of her head and she struggled to sit

up. "I called you Caroline." He stood, pain reminding him of all he'd been through in the past days. Much more and he'd be the one passed out. "Can we…I mean, could we go into the front room? I need to sit. But there's so much I have to tell you."

"And I you." Her face carried a great deal of concern. From what? He was the one with the unbelievable news. But hopefully, news that would bring her peace about her past.

After he settled her in a chair with a knitted shawl over her legs, he drew closer, never allowing the satchel to be out of reach. "Please, you first."

When she looked up, tears squeezed from the corners of her eyes. His heart beat a desperate rhythm in his chest. She was past being upset; fear flickered across her face, causing him to want to pull her into his arms and offer comfort.

"I—"

"Talk to me, Becca." What had her so afraid?

A loud rush of air whooshed from her mouth and Becca had to start over. While her face furrowed into a frown, her foot tapped a steady beat against the wooden floor. "You called me Caroline." She shook her head. "No, let me tell you what I learned and then you can explain that to me."

"All right." He held out a hand, but she drew back.

"I've had some time…" Her fingers twisted together as if she were wringing a chicken's neck. What had her so upset?

"Time for what?"

"Jared. While I was…stuck on the cliff. I dozed off and on. Didn't seem all that real sometimes, but at one point—"

"Yes?"

"At one point, I pictured a family. I remembered. I know it was real, not just a dream. An older man and a woman. A younger man and younger woman."

"Becca—"

"No, listen, please. The younger couple held a beautiful little girl between them. I remember the little girl. I remember sewing clothes for her." Her lids fluttered against the tears. "Jared...I'm married and have a child!"

# Chapter 17

Warm arms surrounded her. She basked in their comfort until the memory returned. "Oh, Jared. I'm so sorry. Don't you see?" She pushed back from him. "I'm married. I have a child. No doubt all of my past will start to come back to me, but for now I'm so sorry for all the trouble I've caused you. You're married to a married woman!"

"I'm what?" He ran a thumb along her jaw. "Of course I'm married to a married woman. You're my wife!"

"I'm already married. We can't be husband and wife. I can't be Mrs. Jared Callahan." She choked on the words. She had to make him understand, but she simply could not bring herself to move out of his embrace.

Jared gazed into her yes. And then he did the unthinkable. He laughed at her. She broke his grasp and rose, hands on hips. He followed, a big smile still firmly in place.

"And what is so funny?" Becca sniffled into a hand-kerchief.

"You aren't married!" She gave him a doubtful glance. "You're not, Becca. That's what I wanted to tell you." He looked bewildered for a second. "Well, you are married, of course, but to me, not like you think."

"What?"

"You'd better sit back down. There's so much to tell you. I hardly know where to begin."

She dabbed at the tears but more fell to take their place. He stretched out a hand and cupped her chin. His touch reached directly to her heart.

"There is nothing to worry about. Let me explain." He shifted his weight from his injured leg. "That Mr. Fletcher—"

"Mr. Fletcher?"

He stroked her face again and she melted against his hand. "Allow me a minute before you get those hackles up."

She stiffened. "I don't raise hackles."

Laughing again, Jared settled next to her. "Oh, you do have hackles, my dear Mrs. Callahan."

He was making fun of her. Becca was no one's Mrs. Anybody. She slapped at his hand.

"And you aren't shy about raising them." His thumb nipped her chin. "Fletcher had some personal items of yours."

"Fletcher? How? Why? Did he find them on the train?"

"Listen, if you keep interrupting me, I'll never finish. I want you to know everything, Becca. I mean… Caroline. You are Caroline Bigby from upstate New

York. According to Fletcher, you and your brother were raised in a small town near a farming area."

*Farmer Spencer.*

"When your parents and sister-in-law passed a few years back from diphtheria, you moved in with your brother to help take care of Lizzie, your niece."

"My niece?" She taunted the edge of her lip. "Lizzie. I have a niece. I can see her. And my parents! I cared for them, didn't I? I do remember." A scowl she couldn't control overcame her face. She should have felt joy, but to remember their passing was painful. "They were all hospitalized, weren't they? Odd we didn't care for them at home."

"Fletcher said half the town was moved into a makeshift hospital. Sounded like you cared for more folks than merely your parents and sister-in-law."

"I suppose that's where I saw splints and the like."

His eyes narrowed. "The what?"

She waved him off. "How does Mr. Fletcher know all of this?"

"He was sitting behind you and another lady on the train. You apparently told her your life story about why you'd left to come West."

"Oh." She bit the edge of her lip. "Well, it doesn't matter right now. But it must all be true. I can remember patients. Some lined against a wall. Others beneath sheets. Like my ma and pa. And then Lizzie's ma. Oh, Jared, it was horrible." Her face fell to her hands. Memories flickered into her mind like one of Mr. Hovenbergh's flip books. First she saw the makeshift hospital. Then the people jammed onto beds, fever and exhaustion scorching their fragile frames. Ma trying to care for Pa when she could barely move herself. "Oh, Jared. I can picture it all now."

His arms encircled her and he whispered against her hair, "You told the lady on the train that you took care of Lizzie until your brother remarried last year. And you wanted to get away, give them a chance to have a life of their own. So you came out here with plans to open your own mercantile. But in a town farther west. You just got off here because of the derailment."

Pictures flashed through her mind. Sitting at a desk, writing letters to see what towns might need what kinds of businesses. "But how did Fletcher get my satchel?"

"When you hit your head and couldn't remember, he pretended to help you so he could take your bag. All the money, your jewelry—"

"Jewelry?" She forced the images into her head. "My mother's brooch! And a necklace. He took them?" Her jaw tightened and she drew back. How dare he take them from her! Those were the last remembrances of the mother she'd lost. And all along she'd thought he was shady. And he'd played the gentleman, even giving her his coat to sit on. Well, of course. He could buy a new one with all the money he'd get from her jewelry.

"Becca...I mean, Caroline. I have them. Here, in the satchel. I have everything but the money, and he'll be paying that back to you when he sells the saloon. You aren't married. You do have a family, and you have... me." He reached for her hand and this time, she didn't pull away. "If you'll still have me, that is. Sounds like you come from some pretty fancy folks."

Fancy folks, like the real Rebecca Layne. How could she bring up the subject of Rebecca? That girl must still be planning a wedding with Jared. "But…what about your…Rebecca? Isn't she going to be arriving one day?"

He shifted. Let go of her hand. "Caroline, I did get a letter from her."

There was no other letter. "You what?"

"Yes. I didn't know how to tell you. She wrote that she couldn't come out. Couldn't give up her good life and the money a wealthy suitor would bring her."

"You knew all along? I was just a fill-in for Rebecca? And you let me believe—"

"No." He reached for her but she stood her ground, then turned around, her back to him. "I just found out. But I was relieved, Caroline."

She slapped her hands together. "Relieved that you were married to the wrong woman? Or relieved that I hadn't intentionally set you up to take care of a helpless woman?" She spun around to confront him. Arms up, ready to do battle, she dared him to admit it. And here she'd thought he was different. Maybe all men were like Mr. Fletcher. Just out for what they could get.

But all he did was grin like a cat with a mouse pinned to the floor. "You didn't *set me up,* Caroline. The minute I saw you I knew you were the only woman I would ever want. Ever. I love you, Caroline, Becca, Rebecca Callahan. My wife."

"Oh, stop calling me Caroline." The only woman ever? Her legs grew wobbly. Did he mean what he said? "Ever? Oh, Jared. I'm just Becca. I'll always be Becca to you." A smile overwhelmed her. She'd be whoever he wanted as long as he loved her.

"Becca, I was relieved when I got Rebecca's letter. I wanted to tell you, but I wasn't sure how you'd react. I had already fallen in love with you."

"You had?" Her heart flipped and fluttered in her chest. All along, that was what she'd longed for and didn't even know it. "I love you, too. So very much." She didn't wait for him to balance on his leg; she threw herself at him.

His lips covered hers. Warm and inviting, he wrapped her in arms that spoke of his caring and protection. She drank in the sweetness of him, his smell, his feel, his strength, all the things she had been afraid to want before. But they were, after all, husband and wife. She slid her arms tighter around his neck and kissed him back.

When he finally opened his eyes and gazed into hers, she understood the desire that reflected from her own. He stepped back. "Whoa, there. Let's do this right. I've waited this long for my beautiful bride, a bit more won't hurt."

Breathless, she gasped. "What do you mean?"

# Epilogue

Becca's brother, Robert, held his arm out for her to take. She placed her fingers lightly on his coat sleeve and smiled into the eyes of a younger version of her father. "Thank you for making the trip out. And for bringing Ma's dress with you."

"Rose and Lizzie wouldn't hear of our not coming. Besides, who would have given you away? I have to tell you how worried we were when we didn't hear back." He leaned over and kissed her forehead. "Now, what shall your big brother call you? Caroline or Becca?"

"You may call me whatever you choose. But to Jared, I'll always be Becca."

They both laughed as Lizzie dashed out in front of them, sprinkling orange and yellow mums along the barn floor.

Becca smiled at the girl's antics. "I'm grateful my

neighbor had flowers left. Said it was odd we haven't had snow yet. What would I have done without flowers?"

He clipped the end of her nose. "With your lovely smile, no one would have noticed. Look ahead. There's your husband, sis. Scared?"

"Well, I wasn't until you said that. He's not really—"

"I know, Caroline. We had a talk. Jared's a good man, a godly man. And I know you'll have a wonderful life here. In fact, Rose and I were talking… Oh, never mind. We can discuss that later."

"What?" Her heart hammered in her chest. Might they…? Then she stared ahead. "You'd better stop talking and walk me down this aisle, big brother. We have a Thanksgiving dinner to eat as soon as this is over."

Jared's smile led her across the straw-filled floor of the barn. Blanche held Becca's flowers while the traveling preacher cleared his throat and opened his Bible.

"…and Caroline Becca Callahan, do you once again take this man…"

She gazed into the patient dark brown eyes of her husband as they repeated the vows, this time for all the world to witness. Her husband! And all of a sudden she simply couldn't wait. Becca tipped onto her toes and kissed him. Then she felt the blush start at her neck and creep over her face as she realized folks were staring. And chuckling.

"Well, there, young lady. I normally tell the young man he may kiss his bride, but you go on ahead. From what I hear, you've waited quite long enough. I pronounce you husband and wife."

The preacher's laugh echoed off the vast barn walls. Mortified by her behavior and his comment, Becca felt her feet frozen to the barn floor. Did the whole town know about their sham of a marriage? Well, of course. They'd no doubt heard how she stayed at Blanche's the past couple of weeks until her family arrived. Her face flamed again. She'd have to get used to the fact that small towns had no secrets.

"Go on, now." The preacher pushed his hands toward them. "You may both kiss each other."

While her family and friends gawked, Jared's arms tightened around her. They were both instantly lost in each other's embrace. His lips sought hers as they never had before, as if searching for the answer to his question. "Do you really love me?"

And she responded with a kiss of her own. "Oh, I certainly do."

Applause rose about them and they looked up, sheepishly remembering where they were.

Breathless, Becca stepped back and searched his face. She drank in the new look in Jared's eyes. A look that told her she would be deeply loved, cherished and cared for by him. Forever.

\* \* \* \* \*

# HEARTSONG

## PRESENTS

Look out for 4 new
Heartsong Presents books next month!

**Every month 4 inspiring faith-filled
romances will be available in stores.**

These contemporary and historical Christian
romances emphasize God's role in every
relationship and reinforce the importance of
faith, hope and love.

# REQUEST YOUR FREE BOOKS!

## 2 FREE CHRISTIAN NOVELS
## PLUS 2
## FREE
## MYSTERY GIFTS

HEARTSONG
PRESENTS

---

**YES!** Please send me 2 Free Heartsong Presents novels and my 2 FREE mystery gifts (gifts are worth about $10). After receiving them, if I don't wish to receive any more books I can return the shipping statement marked "cancel." If I don't cancel, I will receive 4 brand-new novels every month and be billed just $4.24 per book in the U.S. and $5.24 per book in Canada. That's a savings of at least 20% off the cover price. It's quite a bargain! Shipping and handling is just 50¢ per book in the U.S. and 75¢ per book in Canada.* I understand that accepting the 2 free books and gifts places me under no obligation to buy anything. I can always return a shipment and cancel at any time. Even if I never buy another book, the two free books and gifts are mine to keep forever.

159/359 HDN FVYK

| Name | (PLEASE PRINT) | |
|---|---|---|
| Address | | Apt. # |
| City | State | Zip |

Signature (if under 18, a parent or guardian must sign)

### Mail to the **Harlequin®** Reader Service:
### IN U.S.A.: P.O. Box 1867, Buffalo, NY 14240-1867

* Terms and prices subject to change without notice. Prices do not include applicable taxes. Sales tax applicable in N.Y. This offer is limited to one order per household. Not valid for current subscribers to Heartsong Presents books. All orders subject to credit approval. Credit or debit balances in a customer's account(s) may be offset by any other outstanding balance owed by or to the customer. Please allow 4 to 6 weeks for delivery. Offer available while quantities last. Offer valid only in the U.S.

**Your Privacy**—The Harlequin® Reader Service is committed to protecting your privacy. Our Privacy Policy is available online at www.ReaderService.com or upon request from the Harlequin Reader Service.
We make a portion of our mailing list available to reputable third parties that offer products we believe may interest you. If you prefer that we not exchange your name with third parties, or if you wish to clarify or modify your communication preferences, please visit us at www.ReaderService.com/consumerschoice or write to us at Harlequin Reader Service Preference Service, P.O. Box 9062, Buffalo, NY 14269. Include your complete name and address.

HSPDIR13R